ORDERS OF PROTECTION

Previous Winners of the Katherine Anne Porter Prize
in Short Fiction
J. Andrew Briseño, series editor
Barbara Rodman, founding editor

The Stuntman's Daughter by Alice Blanchard
Rick DeMarinis, Judge

Here Comes the Roar by Dave Shaw
Marly Swick, Judge

Let's Do by Rebecca Meacham
Jonis Agee, Judge

What Are You Afraid Of? by Michael Hyde
Sharon Oard Warner, Judge

Body Language by Kelly Magee
Dan Chaon, Judge

Wonderful Girl by Aimee La Brie
Bill Roorbach, Judge

Last Known Position by James Mathews
Tom Franklin, Judge

Irish Girl by Tim Johnston
Janet Peery, Judge

A Bright Soothing Noise by Peter Brown
Josip Novakovich, Judge

Out of Time by Geoff Schmidt
Ben Marcus, Judge

Venus in the Afternoon by Tehila Lieberman
Miroslav Penkov, Judge

In These Times the Home Is a Tired Place by Jessica Hollander
Katherine Dunn, Judge

The Year of Perfect Happiness by Becky Adnot-Haynes
Matt Bell, Judge

Last Words of the Holy Ghost by Matt Cashion
Lee K. Abbott, Judge

The Expense of a View by Polly Buckingham
Chris Offutt, Final Judge

ActivAmerica by Meagan Cass
Claire Vaye Watkins, Final Judge

Quantum Convention by Eric Schlich
Dolan Morgan, Final Judge

Christina:
Thank you so much for
celebrating the launch of this
book with me! ♡ *JH*

ORDERS OF PROTECTION

Jenn Hollmeyer

BY JENN HOLLMEYER

2019 WINNER, KATHERINE ANNE PORTER PRIZE IN SHORT FICTION

UNT PRESS
University of North Texas Press
Denton, Texas

10 9 8 7 6 5 4 3 2 1

Permissions:
University of North Texas Press
1155 Union Circle #311336
Denton, Texas 76203-5017

∞The paper used in this book meets the minimum requirements of the American National Standard for Permanence of Paper for Printed Library Materials, z39.48.1984. Binding materials have been chosen for durability.

Library of Congress Cataloging-in-Publication Data

Names: Hollmeyer, Jenn, 1977– author.
Title: Orders of protection / Jenn Hollmeyer.
Description: First edition. | Denton : University of North Texas Press,
  [2019] | Series: Katherine anne porter prize in short fic; number 18 |
Identifiers: LCCN 2019024392 | ISBN 9781574417753 (paperback) | ISBN
  9781574417852 (ebook)
Classification: LCC PS3608.O488 A6 2019 | DDC 813/.6—dc23
LC record available at https://lccn.loc.gov/2019024392

Orders of Protection is Number 18 in the Katherine Anne Porter Prize in Short Fiction Series

The electronic edition of this book was made possible by the support of the Vick Family Foundation.

For Dell and Eleanor

Contents

Orders of Protection

When you accept the job, your friends say you're selfless. Then they say you're a fool. They laugh and tell stories about their bosses and buy you Manhattans at the Legal Bar, a place you'll never afford on your salary, but you don't mind. The cherries taste like bronchitis and the napkin feels like your mother's hand.

∼

On your first day, a coneflower of a woman walks into your office and asks who the hell you are. You say you're her new attorney, and the petals of her dress wilt with disappointment. You look like a Girl Scout. When she sits down, she tells you about the man who beats her, that he looks like the nicest guy in the world, like he'd be your dentist or your mailman or your cousin, you know? You say you know.

∼

At home that night you want to remember being a child, so you sit on the fire escape with a bag of candies that change flavor as you suck on them. Grape becomes strawberry, lime becomes orange, and banana becomes armpit. Then you realize the last one has always tasted this way, not just since you put it in your mouth but since twenty years ago. None of the flavors have ever tasted how they should, and nothing ever changes, not really. Your tongue feels like your cat's. You drop the rest of the candies through the grate and wait for someone on the sidewalk to look up at you, but no one does.

∼

You're in the courtroom, waiting for the coneflower woman, when the judge starts to make small talk, which with him is never small. He says people only do what you do for three reasons. One, there aren't any other jobs. Two, they're religious. Or three, they can identify with their clients because they've had hard lives themselves. He doesn't ask which reason applies to you, and you don't say. Your client walks in the door, wearing a black dress and a black eye.

~

One of your friends calls and asks how it's going, what it's like to be selfless. You hear the word "selfish" and a spear of heat rises up your spine and fills your face. You're afraid you've missed a voicemail or a birthday, and you say you're sorry, you're so sorry, and she laughs, thinking you're being ironic, and you realize your mistake and you laugh, too. So, what *is* it like to be selfless, to lose yourself in your work? You try to think of an answer, but the silence says it for you.

~

A woman with a voice like wool calls and asks for an emergency order. You tell her to come in right away. An hour goes by. Then two, then three. The receptionist goes to lunch and comes back smelling like Saturday night. You call the wool woman and no one answers, so you think she's on her way. Your stomach growls. At five o'clock a woman walks in and you ask if she's the emergency, and she says yes. She twirls around and you look for blood or bruises, but all you see is layers of scarves and cardigans and price tags. I had to go shopping, she says. A little re-*tail* therapy. She says it like that, putting the emphasis on the tail, and you can't help but look at her ass with the triple-digit figure. You ask if she's sure she qualifies for your services, and she says of course she does. She needs help with a man. He mean, she says. You ask to hear the story, what he does, and how much evidence she has. She leans forward and says oh, I got evidence. He yell at me, he scream, he mean.

~

You were five the last time you called someone mean, and the someone was the person who was supposed to protect you. When you said the word she became the kind of mean the wool woman has never known. You think of faces changing shape, voices changing tone, hands changing intent and then going right back to what they were. You think of playrooms and toy chests and tree houses and all of that changing to nothing, and then a moment later someone saying again how lucky you are, how fortunate, how blessed. Even now you feel the price of those words, and you know you must get rid of anything that reminds you of how much you paid for it, even the handbag you got for five dollars and the plastic ring from the gumball machine. You spend the weekend sorting everything you own, and by Sunday night you've stuffed your life into seven garbage bags. You take them to Goodwill, and when you get back you give yourself a tour of the place that costs two-thirds of what you make every month. Here is the bedroom with the milk-crate nightstand. Here is the bathroom with the single toothbrush. Here is the living space with the secondhand couch and stale kitchenette. Even this is more than you need. You wonder if you should have donated your TV, your cat, your food. You stare at the contents of your refrigerator for so long you feel guilty for wasting energy, and you realize that you are the opposite of selfless, that who you are has taken hold of you, and what you need more than anything is an order of protection against yourself.

~

A woman dressed like an icicle is waiting in your office on Monday morning. She talks about property lines and tree limbs and loud parties and demands protection from her neighbor. You ask where she lives, and she gives an address on the side of town where they build houses like club sandwiches, stacked high and held together with weather vanes. But she is not rich. She has lost her job and her car and now her neighbor has stolen her garden shears, and she's afraid she'll wake up with a rose bush embedded in her chest. You ask if maybe the neighbor thought the garden shears were hers, or if she was just borrowing them for a while, or if maybe the icicle woman misplaced them and the neighbor didn't take them after all. She stares at you. Whose side are you on? she asks. There is a property line marked with stones, and my side is on the right. I fear for my life, she says, and you can see this is somehow true. You want to tell her a story about real fear, about hearing a sound in the night and looking for safety and finding nothing but empty beds and unlocked doors and your dog bleeding in the street and so scared itself that every time you call, it runs farther away from you. This woman's handbag and ring look like the ones you just gave away, and you think you must be imagining things, and you are. Still, you pretend they used to be yours, that you know nothing about dogs or blood or night, and finally you can feel those garden shears closing around your nipple, the one on the right, the blades cold and sticky with sap. You ask the icicle woman to tell you more.

~

Your friends say let me buy you a drink. Let me bring you a napkin. Let me tell you a story. They talk about a boy who moved into their neighborhood and how they stalked him to and from the coffee shop every morning for a week until a girl leaned out of his bedroom window and yelled, and they got embarrassed and ran away laughing and spilling five-dollar lattes down their hundred-dollar dresses. Then they ask how things are going with your job, whether you're looking for something that pays more. You say no. But you tell them about the coneflower woman who left the courthouse yesterday with her arm around the man whose photograph you keep in a folder about her restraining order, which she has asked the court to dissolve because she loves him after all. Then you tell them about the wool woman and the icicle woman, and how you lost both cases, but the judge commended you for trying. Your clients don't need to win; they just need someone to stand up for them. This is what you think and when the judge says the same thing out loud, you know he knows your reason for taking this job. Your friends laugh. They ask how you can spend so much time on things that don't matter. You think of rich boys and jealous girls, and you think of garden shears, mean men, and the kind of concealer that will hide a black eye.

This time, you say, let me tell you a story about myself, and you make them listen.

A Thousand Needle Stings

I came home from work one night and found Herrisch strutting in circles with a hair comb stuck in her feathers. She's our alpha hen—her name means "bossy" in German— and she was kicking her raw-looking feet in fits of humiliation. There's some irony here, the hen wearing a comb like a rooster when the rooster was dead. It took ten minutes to corner her and set her free.

As I walked back to the house, Berndt appeared at the door and asked if he should call the kids to help me.

"I got it," I said, waving the comb.

He cupped his palm around the stub that used to be his other arm, and I turned away. "Any news?" he asked, meaning my office job at Well-Chem, which the employees called Hell-Chem, the way they used to call Miss Horace Miss Whore Ass in high school. Many of them had never left Fulton County, except for school trips to Chicago and Springfield.

"Safe for now." I would wait until later to tell him about the twelve who got let go.

The next night, it was jingle bells. Someone had pulled them off the Christmas wreath and made a necklace for Komisch— German for "funny." She sounded like a reindeer pecking in the yard.

I wouldn't have minded or even questioned any of this—with four kids, there's a lot you don't question—except the elementary school had called and said Cassie was doing the same types of things to Edward Hopper, the class rabbit. Last week she'd put rubber bands on its tail, and now she'd tied a scarf around its ears. It made me uncomfortable to imagine the teachers talking about my youngest daughter. Some of them had been my teachers, too, and probably still thought of me as the dreamy, inattentive girl I'd once been.

"We think this is about Felicia," the teacher told me on the phone. "Cassie's strange behavior started right after she died." The teacher was new, just out of college, and you could tell she didn't have children of her own.

"Have any of the other kids been acting—funny?" I asked.

"No, but Cassie had a special connection with Felicia."

I nodded as if I knew, as if the woman could see me. Cassie hadn't mentioned Felicia until the tumor was public knowledge, and even then she didn't talk about her much. For months the teacher forwarded health updates to the parents, and for another few weeks after Felicia stopped coming to school. The whole town attended the funeral, and it was as horrible as you'd expect, but I didn't think Cassie had a *special connection*. If anyone did, it was my son, Jacob, and his connection was to the dead girl's sister. He'd taken her to the winter formal.

The teacher kept talking. "You probably know Cassie has an imaginary friend now—"

"She's always had one." It was her way of compensating for the bond between her twin sisters.

"—named Felicia." The teacher paused. "Cassie said Felicia put the scarf on the rabbit."

The chickens were Berndt's idea. He'd grown up on a farm in Germany, and said they made him feel more at home here in Crestfall, Illinois. Plus, he could feed them and collect their eggs with one hand. He said it was the only job he could manage now, and I said no, that isn't true. He said well, this was the least he could do, and I agreed with that.

He'd turned the chicken coop into a family project. Before the accident, I would have urged him to hire someone instead. I'd always favored handymen, babysitters, and paying extra for assembly and installation. But he liked us to do things on our own, and once he mentioned something in front of the kids, there was no turning back. That's how we ended up bringing our kids on our tenth anniversary trip to Memphis, and it's how we ended up with mismatched legs on our brand-new dining room table—Berndt cracked the originals while screwing them in with the wrong drill bit, the kids sitting around him, helping.

Financially, do-it-yourself was our only option now, even though Berndt could do less for himself than ever before. But while sealing our own driveway and patching our own roof would save money, producing our own eggs would not. In fact, it would cost us. I didn't realize this until after Berndt downloaded a blueprint and ordered the lumber, and by then it was too late. The twins, Rachel and Robyn, had already sketched a paint motif of ringed planets that looked like fried eggs, which I found disturbing but also clever. So, for four weekends straight last spring, Jacob and I measured and sawed and hammered, while Berndt and the three girls turned the structure into a galaxy for our back-ordered flock of Red Stars, Black Stars, and White Giants.

If I stood on Berndt's left side while he rolled paint onto the wood, I couldn't see his stump. I could almost forget for a while.

When the twenty-five chicks arrived in the mail, I dug out my old German textbook and started looking for names. Chapter three was all about opposites, and the exercise at the end asked you to pick which word describes the cartoon above it. Gut oder schlecht? Glücklich oder traurig? Faul oder fleißig? The last one was my favorite because you could tell it was the Germans' favorite, too: Lazy or industrious? They emphasized this question over all the others, giving it its own page and a larger font, as if they wanted you to consider the lifelong implications. The picture showed a fat kid slumped in a chair—definitely faul, which I spelled "foul" and sometimes "fowl," which is why I barely passed the course. The Germans wanted you to be fleißig, a skinny kid furiously scribbling in a notebook—spelling correctly, no doubt—a word so efficient, the two S's ran together and became one symbol.

We tried to be efficient. We reused paper towels, watered down the kids' milk, wore our clothes a few extra times between washings. But Berndt's disability check wasn't enough. My paycheck wasn't enough. And selling eggs in the break room at work wasn't enough.

I'd killed Fleißig first, out of spite. It had taken me all of Christmas break to work up the nerve, but it wasn't so bad once I caught her. She made a stringy divan and a gamey soup. The rooster—Schwartzie—had died next, but that was the coyote's doing, not mine. I needed to replace him, or at least order more chicks, or we'd run out of meat before long.

Komisch would be next. I'd remove the head first, then the jingle bells.

I tried talking to Cassie about Felicia while the chicken pot pie cooled on the stove. I got as far as asking how she liked her teacher these days, and then the front door slammed and in walked Jacob with Felicia's sister, Marcy. She's one of those girls who looks like a spoon—concave and silver-plated. Jacob was a knife standing next to her.

"She's staying for dinner," he said, straightening his posture and daring me to fight him on it. I had a rule that the family had to eat together, and when Berndt went on disability I'd made a second rule about not inviting friends to eat with us. But Jacob didn't have many friends, and Marcy was the first girl he'd brought home.

"You're always welcome here," I told her. It was something another mom would say. Jacob's eyes narrowed. He was always calling me out on sounding fake. But I couldn't help it. It had been a tough year. I was trying to make up for it.

"How've you been doing, Marcy?" I asked, the words coming slowly. "And your parents?"

"Okay, I guess." She rested her fist on the counter, trying to look casual.

It's strange talking to someone you met at a funeral, when her face was streaked and sallow. I'd seen pictures since then, of course, from the winter formal—Jacob in Berndt's tweed jacket and a second-hand tie that matched his gray eyes, Marcy a foot shorter in a strapless dress the color of wasabi. I'd asked if they were dating, and he'd glared at me.

I put an extra plate on the counter for Marcy—I don't set tables—and told her what we were having, afraid there wouldn't be enough. I called upstairs for Berndt and the girls, feeling as I often did that he was one of them now—and that the shadow in the corner was not Jacob, but a non-load-bearing part of the architecture.

"I don't eat meat," Marcy said, and I felt relieved for the first time in months.

They say one of the most humane ways to kill a chicken is to turn it upside down and wait for it to get disoriented. Then slit its throat, let the blood drain out, and put it in ice water. I do it at night behind the shed so no one sees.

I'm holding Glücklich by her feet, waiting for the nerves to stop twitching, when Jacob comes out of the woods. He stops when he sees me there with my camping lantern and puts the joint behind his back. It's warm for February. He's only wearing a sweatshirt with his jeans.

"I was wondering where that smell was coming from," I say. "Must be nice to have money for that."

"I have a job."

I've gone so far as to ask Berndt if we should take a cut of Jacob's snow-shoveling and lawn-mowing money. We could do it as a loan and pay him back when things get better. But he said no, and he's right. I know that.

Jacob is so much like Berndt—that same cool distance—it scares me. I want him to be careful. To slow down. Take deep breaths. I will say these words if he asks about the chicken, and whether we're going to be okay, if we'll make it or not. But he doesn't ask. He pinches the end of the joint and walks back to the house. He's a man now, broad in the shoulders, yet he will eat his dinner and sleep in his bed and not think about what tomorrow will bring. I want to scream at him for taking it all for granted. For thinking I'd let him get away with the pot, but also for making me waste energy punishing him when there are bigger problems to solve.

But when he pauses at the door, I can see that he is already thinking about tomorrow, that he knows about the bigger problems, and my anger drains into this bucket of blood at my feet.

Marcy started showing up at dinnertime a couple nights a week. She brought her own food, in baggies—baby carrots, grapes, dried apricots—things that represent body parts in children's Halloween games. Fingers, eyeballs, ears. I wondered if this was her lunch and what then, if anything, she ate in the middle of the day.

I'd started skipping lunch myself because they'd cut my hours at work. They only needed someone to answer phones in the mornings now. When I left each day at noon, I recorded an outgoing message with the date and our signature sign-off: "Keeping you well at Well-Chem." The first day they told me to do it again and try to sound cheerful. So I did. Good enough, they said.

At dinnertime, Rachel and Robyn sat with me at the table, scribbling notes to each other on a napkin, and Cassie and Jacob ate next to Marcy on the floor by the TV. I used to have a rule about not watching it during meals, but I'd stopped caring. Eating was easier with a laugh track. Jacob and Berndt stared at the screen, opposing forces in the room—the boy steady as a stone while his father wobbled through dinner, cutting his meat with a fork on a rickety tray table. Cassie moved closer to Marcy to get out of his way.

"Maybe Marcy doesn't want you leaning on her while she eats," I said. Cassie turned her wide eyes up to me. She was wearing one of my old Save the Ales T-shirts, only slightly too big on her.

"It's all right," Marcy said, and Cassie pressed against her. Cassie had never acted like this with anyone else, not even her sisters. I worried that Cassie would say something about Felicia, or start talking to the air, but she kept quiet, aside from complimenting Marcy's chain-link earrings and wire shoelaces. I watched Cassie, and Cassie watched Marcy, and an amazing thing happened—Marcy put her arm around my daughter and squeezed. Marcy's sleeve lifted along her onion-colored skin, and there it was—a mottled bruise. A shadow of a hand. You could see the marks where fingers had dug into her bicep. My heart skipped a beat. No wonder she'd rather eat old grapes on our living room floor than go home to her family.

On Saturday morning I watched Berndt feed the chickens. He looked like an old man, bending to the bucket in his faded trench coat, slinging corn and leftover spaghetti across the dead grass. Like the men in the park he never wanted to become—the ones who fed pigeons outside his old apartment in Chicago. We used to sit on his balcony with mugs of coffee and watch them, wondering what it would be like to live your whole life in one city block. I was the one who made him move to Crestfall and build this house. It was either that or give up my parents' land. He said he didn't mind, said it was like the place he'd grown up, but he didn't have to tell me he wasn't ready to go back to that. He was a man who needed his circle to swing wide for decades before returning to the point where it had begun.

Looking back, the accident seemed inevitable. He hadn't known how to live with two arms in this town. He'd kept as busy as possible with car repairs, poker, fishing, shuffleboard, and hunting, but he was always looking for more to do. Once he lost his right arm, he let the left one hang at his side. If I'd known that was the way to keep him home, I would have bought my butcher knife years ago.

We had three hundred dollars and three chickens. Schlecht, Faul, and Traurig. Bad, Lazy, and Sad. So it all came down to this. Would things have been better if I'd saved Happy for last? Was it any surprise that Sad always cowered in the corner, out of my reach?

"Does it seem like we have fewer chickens?" I asked Berndt one morning. I couldn't believe he hadn't figured out where his meat was coming from, what I went through to keep this family going.

"Jacob told me you're killing them." He was trying to separate a coffee filter from the stack. He didn't look at me.

I would not be denied. "Does it *seem* like fewer?"

He threw the crown of filters across the room. I should have picked them up. He should have let me make the coffee in the first place.

"Felicia is sick of chicken," Cassie said from the living room. She was forcing a piece into place on Berndt's jigsaw puzzle. Rachel and Robyn were doing homework on the couch, each wearing one earbud, an iPod between them on the cushion.

"I didn't know Felicia was still with us," I said.

"She wants you to paint her nails."

I studied the flat plane of Cassie's face. Then I found my little case of years-old, gloppy polish and let her pick colors for the three of us. She lined them up along the knobby edge of partially constructed sky. It was going to be a picture of the sandhill crane migration. I'd seen it in person once, in some marsh in Indiana, many years ago—all those hollow-boned creatures, knowing exactly what to do to survive.

I looked up halfway through Cassie's second hand and saw Marcy standing in the doorway. She seemed to live here now.

"How've you been doing, Marcy?" I asked. "And your parents?" I was incapable of real conversation.

"Pick a color," Cassie said. I expected Marcy to make an excuse and disappear, but she came and sat with us. She rooted around in the case and set a bottle of steely gray on the wing of a crane.

"The purple is for Felicia," Cassie said, and I held my breath.

"She liked blue better," Marcy said.

Midnight. I sit in the corner of the kitchen with a bottle of cheap wine, a stack of bills, and the checkbook, balancing. Teetering. The stove light my only hint that I'm awake, and not sure I believe it. I pinch my arm and my arm pinches back. Even this has become a fight.

Footsteps fall on the stairs leading from the basement. Two sets. A new nightmare. But no one would want to break into our house. No flat screens. No jewelry. No.

Door opens and it's a spoon and a knife. Scoop and slice. She shouldn't be here this late. Shouldn't be doing what she must be doing with my son. Flash of Marcy bringing home a baby, more people with nowhere to go, nothing to do, nothing but time. It's heavy, the weight of so much absence. Missing money, missing arm, missing chickens, rabbit, girl. Teacher said Edward Hopper's old and might die and he did, and now Cassie wears her scarf every day at school, at home, in bed. She is doing whatever she can to hold on to the pieces of her life, but life keeps prying back her fingers, and this is the cruelest of cruel. But there is no humane way to survive.

He is touching her.

I should tell them I'm here so they know, but it's too late, too weird. I look away.

"Stop it," she says. I've never heard her say anything but a verbal shrug.

His hand is under her shirt now, and she says stop again. She cannot raise her voice without getting them both in trouble. She will protect him, and he knows this. I can see it in his profile, the way his mouth opens and his lip trembles and he catches it in his teeth. He grabs her arm above the elbow. He twists the skin. He shakes his wrist and she gasps and I am her and he is Berndt with two arms and we are standing in the back of Jimmy's Tavern and I'm already thinking of ways to cover up the bruise so my mother won't see.

He never hit me. That was the thing. It was always a squeeze, both of his hands on both of my arms. A hug gone hard. It started with a story or a joke and he'd laugh, but I'd take it too far and the anger exploded like bang snaps on the sidewalk of my skin.

Some kid threw those at Jacob in elementary school one time. As proof, Jacob brought home the spent explosives and held them out to us like popcorn.

"So I gave him a snakebite," he said.

"I don't know what that is," Berndt said.

Jacob shoved the snaps back in his pocket and put both hands on his father's arm—the one he would later lose—and twisted in opposite directions, just enough to show what it could do.

"Where I come from, that's called a thousand needle stings, and it hurts worse than any snakebite. The key is what you call it," Berndt said. "Next time, give him one of those and he'll leave you alone for good."

I made chicken teriyaki with rice. No vegetables. No appetite. I cut up the chicken that was on my plate and divided it between Rachel and Robyn.

Marcy was in her usual spot on the floor in front of the TV, hiding behind her bent knees. Cassie leaned against Marcy, and their closeness made me sweat in spite of the snow swirling outside the window behind them. I didn't know what I'd do if Cassie ended up like this girl, quiet and sitting on someone's dirty carpet, picking room-temperature carrots out of a wet baggie. I wanted to roll up her sleeves and put my hands over her bruises, like cupping fireflies in the yard. I wanted to twist the skin on Jacob's arm, break the bone, bring him to weakness like his father. The urge was more than I could stand.

I pushed my chair back and stood up. "Marcy, I think it would be better if you ate dinner at your house from now on," I said.

"What?" Jacob asked, twisting against the couch. "Why?"

"Your family must miss you."

"What are you doing?" Berndt asked. I was surprised to hear his voice.

"Fine," Jacob said. "We'll both leave." He stood up, slid his empty plate on the coffee table and pulled Marcy out of the room. Cassie looked like she'd been pushed down. The door slammed.

"Don't you like her?" Berndt asked.

"I do, I just —" Cassie glared at me, and the lie took shape as I said it. "Her mom called and said she wants her to come home. It must be lonely there." I sat back down.

"Well, you got what you wanted," Berndt said. "One less mouth to feed."

I started to protest—no, it's not that, she doesn't even eat our food—but I stopped short. He meant Jacob.

Everyone said there would be another round of layoffs at Well-Chem, but no one guessed it would happen the way it did. There was a small crowd outside when I showed up for work one morning, their chatter making clouds in the cold. I figured the fire alarm had gone off, or the accounting clerk was showing the smokers more pictures of her grandbaby. When they told me the news, I had to see for myself. I recognized my boss' handwriting on the cardboard taped to the door. *Notice: We have closed for business.* That was it. There had been rumors that Dow might buy us, or some of us might have to go work for Chapman in Peoria, but that's an hour away and no one wanted to work in a plant that smelled like a hog farm.

I didn't wait to hear more. I drove home the long way, past empty storefronts, foreclosures, Cassie's elementary school, the twins' middle school, and the high school where I pictured Jacob sulking at a desk. He came home late every night now and went straight to his room in the basement, even when I called him. He wouldn't speak to me. The one time I put my hand on his arm, he jerked away. Don't touch me, he said, gritting his teeth, and I let go. He'd been gone for years.

I drove through the neighborhood behind the school, past the little gray house where I took singing lessons from a lady at our church when I was a teenager. An older couple lived there now. I'd seen them once, reading the paper on the porch. Today it looked like no one was home. I wanted to sit in that wicker rocker by the door and wait for them, ask if I could have a piece of cake or a slice of pie. I would have killed for some decadence, or even just a song.

I woke up with something pinching the skin under my eye. I had slept on the couch again, waiting up for Jacob, but either I missed him or he never came home. The knot in my back felt like a hot saucepan. I rubbed my face, and my fingers came away with stickers. Red and yellow stars that smelled like bubble gum.

The next morning it was a macaroni necklace, the one Cassie had made in preschool, sagging on my head like a halo. I felt like a dead chicken. Or a dead rabbit.

She was alone in the living room, between the ghosts of Marcy and Felicia, watching someone redecorate a million-dollar house on TV. I knelt beside her and pulled her close and sat with her for a long time.

"I'm not going anywhere," I told her.

I kill fowl.

I kill Faul on a Friday. The end of laziness. The last of my excuses. It would be easy to keep blaming someone else, or the whole situation, and to point to all the ways I stay busy. But the real problem is, I don't know how to be the strong one. And I don't know how to let Berndt be the strong one, either. Somehow, we have to learn to take turns, to find balance between extremes.

He's dozing on the couch, and I shake his stump to wake him. It's the first time I've touched it since it healed, since I removed the last bandage, and it's embarrassing.

"Come help," I say.

He doesn't ask with what. He just follows me into the kitchen. I pull Faul's body from the sink and offer her up. He takes the carcass by the feet, and I show him how to scald it in the pot of boiling water on the stove. Up and down to loosen the feathers. Then he puts it back in the sink and we pluck. It's like the old days when we bathed our babies here. The fatty white skin feels clammy but also warm to the touch. Like diaper rash.

"We need to order more chicks," I say. "We can afford it with my last paycheck."

"We shouldn't name them," he says. He studies the reddish brown feathers between his fingers. They're the color of Cassie's hair.

It's a quiet night. The girls have gone to bed. Their Kit-Cat clock ticks away the seconds.

Berndt holds the chicken steady on the cutting board while I remove the feet, head, and oil gland. I want him to be impressed, and he is. He steps back, holding his hand away from his clothes, and watches while I pull out the guts, careful not to rupture the gall bladder or intestines. I put the bloody parts in a garbage bag, tie it shut, and lower Faul into a pot of ice water.

"What are we going to do?" I ask, looking from the bird to Berndt. Outside, the spotlight casts a blue light on the empty chicken coop.

"Place the order," he says.

"I will," I say. "If you talk to Jacob."

Berndt shrugs and shakes his head. He's afraid he's forgotten how to be a father.

"No, really," I say, and I take his fouled hand between mine. "He'll only listen to you. He's just like you were at that age."

His reflex, even now, is to pull away. But I hold on, and he relaxes. I can see he knows exactly what I'm talking about, and his face fogs over.

I run warm water in the sink. I rub soap into his knuckles and around and under his nails where a year's worth of dirt has collected. His skin feels dead. This palm, a wing. These fingers, legs. This act, not a kindness, but another necessity for survival, and part of me hopes the girls wake up and wander in here to see. We stand there together until the water turns cold.

Another Round

On the night the lead singer of Punk Button turned sixty somewhere in London, his impersonator celebrated with a sheet cake in Aurora, Illinois. The black icing read, "Here's to Another Round." Another Round was the name of the tribute band as well as Punk Button's 1979 hit single, the one with the drum intro that fucks with your heart rhythm.

John cut the cake himself. He wasn't going to do candles or any of that shit, but the bartender stuck a cherry on a toothpick in the first dozen pieces while the crowd sang. "Happy birthday, dear Surge, happy birthday to you." They said he didn't look a day over fifty-nine. John said thanks, even though he was only fifty-four. His girlfriend, Maria, laughed because she was forty-nine.

He turned away from the bar with a beer and almost collided with a man holding a corner piece on a napkin.

"I could use a fork," the guy said.

John looked around the bar and shrugged. Everyone else was eating with their fingers, like a bunch of overgrown kids. He tried to keep moving, but the guy stopped him.

"You don't recognize me," he said. "And you're the one who looks so different." He smiled and lifted his chin a few smug degrees.

John squinted at the beefy man's pinched, pockmarked features. Gray eyes too small, too close together. Hair too shaggy. Not in a punk way, but in a messy, forgotten way. Something about him looked familiar, but John shook his head. "Did we play together at Fan Fest?"

"You played in a band with my big brother."

It took him a second before he remembered. The brother was Wes Jones, lead vocalist and guitarist of The Izz, the slamming garage band of Jamison Court in southeast Aurora. For three years in the early '70s, John and Wes jammed almost every afternoon with two other guys while Wes' weird brother sulked around in the basement, building shitty racecars and robots out of scrap wood and hammered pop cans. All the kids used to call him Fang. The old name almost slipped out, but John caught himself. "You're Frank Jones! Jesus." He meant Jesus, I thought you would have ended up in prison. But he said, "It's been too long."

John expected a thumping embrace or at least a handshake to mark the relief of remembering who the hell he was. But Frank remained cool and distant in his plain white T-shirt.

John started to reach for Maria's elbow, to introduce her to this old buddy-who-wasn't-really, but then he thought who the hell cares. She was busy talking to the other band girlfriends anyway. Well, she was the only girlfriend; the others were all wives.

Frank held his cake away from his body, as if his dog had shat it. "So what's this like?" he asked.

"This? Being Surge? It's fun."

"I bet. You got the hair, the Chucks, the black leather jacket—it'd be great to see you play sometime."

"We're working on a national tour." John ran his fingers through his hair the way Surge did, twice in succession, followed by a slight shake of his head. It had taken him years to perfect that move. "But for now we're playing street fairs. First one is tomorrow night, and they run through Ribfest." He said it like they played Ribfest every year, like they hadn't been hoping for a shot at that gig for as long as he could remember. John dug around in his pocket. "I'm out of cards, but just go to punk another round dot com. The tour calendar's up there."

Frank repeated the web address like a mantra and then stood staring at John. The silence grew awkward and made John think of puberty and curfews and stale Cheetos. He mumbled something about old times and wishing he could talk more, but he needed to get ready for the next day's show.

"Happy birthday," Frank said, holding out a hand smeared with frosting.

The first show of the summer felt like the last day of school, with that same anything-can-happen feeling. John always took the day off from Pop's Vending and arrived early to watch the town set up. He'd buy a couple red hots and look on while the police barricaded the road, smirking at the first car that couldn't turn where it wanted to. There was usually a pause while the driver nudged forward to see if Main Street was actually closed—Really? Could it be?—and then the police officer pointed for him to just fucking go straight and turn at the next block instead. It was a commanding, celebratory sort of gesture, this finger-pointing. We're in charge, and we get to tell you where to drive.

And it was all because of Surge.

He was important enough to interrupt the flow of traffic. Because *he* was *Surge*! The realization never got old. John felt the sculpted bulge of his jaw as he chewed, the measured way he blinked his eyes under the fringe of precisely dyed hair, the pull of the old Media Sound T-shirt across his stomach. He. Was. *Surge*.

And this was Daisy Days. How lame could you get. It made him think of cartoon cows wearing straw hats. Maria thought it was cute, and this was the only show his mother would have come to if she were still alive, if that tells you anything. The real Surge used to play the Roundhouse and the Rainbow Theatre in London, but John played on a temporary stage in the middle of a one-block suburban downtown lined with faux nostalgia. An old-time ice cream shop, a vintage clothing store, a garage that specialized in servicing classic cars. In this context, the banner advertising the week-long festival lineup made Another Round sound like a repeat. Just another round of music everyone's already heard. Sometimes his whole life felt that way.

"I'm not doing this show ever again. This place is like a set for a sitcom," John said when the rest of the guys from the band arrived.

"You say that every year, and then they pay us," Mike said, hoisting his guitar out of the truck. "Ribfest will be here before you know it."

They were good guys, these three. He had to remind himself of that because although they'd been playing together for years, they didn't know each other all that well outside of the music. He knew Mike had a grown kid in California, Paul had Hep C, and Dave worked some kind of office job in his real life. But otherwise, they were interchangeable in their generic black jeans and black T-shirts. They could have been any of the various guitarists and drummers that had played for Punk Button over the years. Hell, these guys could have been the ones from The Izz. You'd never know the difference.

The Izz. Shit. He hadn't thought about Wes and those guys in years.

A few minutes past seven, Dave hit the drums and led them into "Another Round." It was kind of a toned-down D-beat, but it still ripped through you, reverberating off the storefronts. They might not know each other well off the stage, but on it they knew everything—which cue meant what and how to play in a way that would make Punk Button proud. They picked over the bridge pickup. They kept the treble high. They fucking railed.

"Another round, this lost and found, feels like drowwwn-ing . . ." John sang, forming the words at the front of his mouth to get that tinny, buzzy Surge sound. "The same old song, gone on too long, what the hell went wronnng . . ."

Maria put her fingers in her mouth and whistled, jumping up and down in her white nurse shoes, loyal as ever, even though she kept saying she was ready to put this phase of their life behind them. Do something else with their time. Maybe even get married after all these years.

As Mike started the intro to "Living the Dream," John spotted an eager grin a few yards away. He squinted and frowned. Fang. Frank. John didn't think the guy was serious about coming, much less that he'd come right away to the first show.

Frank waved. Just a slight shake of two fingers, like summoning a waiter. From this distance, he looked to be about twenty years old. Maybe because he had a round face. And you couldn't see the pockmarks from his acne unless you were standing close. He'd gotten a haircut since last night, but it was still shaggy and shapeless, as if he'd done it himself. Shit, it was how Wes used to wear his hair. The guy had grown up just enough to look like Wes did as an upperclassman.

"Living the dreeeam," John sang, "the one that makes you screeeam."

It was like the 1979 Finger on the Button Tour all over again, when John and Wes saw Punk Button play in Chicago. Except this time, John was on stage and the Wes look-alike was in the crowd. But Wes had never come to see Another Round. All these years of local gigs, and Wes had never come once. John expected as much of his father, but Wes used to love Punk Button. He absolutely idolized Surge back in the day. Wes collected every album, every newspaper photograph and every article about him that ran in *The Chord*.

A glint caught John's eye—something shiny in Frank's hand. A shoebox-sized gift wrapped in aluminum foil. John didn't realize it was for him until after the show, when Frank showed up at

Tracy's Tavern and set it on the table, like a cat bringing his master a dead rodent.

"You do know yesterday wasn't *my* birthday."

Frank scraped a stool up to the table, and John reluctantly introduced him to everyone as a friend from high school.

"I want to hear what John was like back then," Maria said, pouring glasses of 312 from a pitcher.

"He was my brother's little sidekick. Followed him around like a puppy."

John could see Frank's pockmarks now, the way they turned his skin into a pudding. "You and I didn't know each other that well," John said.

"Sure we did. You were at my house every day."

"Your brother and I riffed and smoked joints in your dad's shed, but *you* weren't around much."

"You two were more like brothers than he and I ever were." The truth of this statement passed like a searchlight across Frank's face. "But I got the *Finger on the Button* album before either of you did."

Frank had taken three city buses to get to the nearest record store that carried punk. When he got home, he locked himself in Wes' bedroom and played the music just loud enough for his own ears, leaving the other two straining and pounding at the door until they broke a hole in it.

"You didn't even like punk," John said.

"Bought it just to make you mad." Frank's boyish face twisted into a pink smirk. After all these years he was still glad he'd pulled that one off. John didn't remind him that after school the next day, Wes got back at Frank by locking him out of the house in the snow.

Frank pointed to the box. "Open it."

John peeled the foil back like the fingers of a fist. The shoebox inside looked like it had been used in a pet's funeral long ago.

He almost said he hoped it was one of Frank's old pop-can robot creations, but he didn't want to be a complete jackass.

He looked closer and saw the Converse logo. Men's size ten. Wes' size. He opened the lid, expecting to see the ratty old shoes, but it was like finding a long-ago ex-girlfriend's underwear under the bed. He unearthed the scent of stale cigarette smoke and more glinting—safety pins. About a thousand of them in neat rows attached to a faded black T-shirt in true punk style. It had taken weeks to fasten them side-by-side, all in the shape and position of the human torso's bones—ribs, spine, and collarbone—to look like a skeleton. John and Wes had each made one to wear at every official Izz show.

"This one's yours, right?" Frank asked. "It was with all the band stuff at my parents' house."

John nodded and fingered the tag where he'd written his name. "Wes had one just like it." He remembered how the shirts made them into real punk stars, the lights flashing against the pins like x-rays. "How *is* Wes? I haven't talked to that bastard in years."

Frank didn't answer, and John looked up.

"I thought you knew." Frank raised his eyebrows and took a sip of his beer. "He died a couple months ago."

John wasn't sure he'd heard right, but the bar wasn't that noisy.

"Heart attack. He was working too hard."

"Shit." John slumped back. "No, I didn't know."

"That's why I'm here. I've been in Saint Louis since college, but I moved back to help my parents for a while."

John folded the shirt, remembering Mrs. Jones' chalky elbows and Mr. Jones' guitar-string eyebrows. Their willingness to park the car in the driveway so Wes could keep the instruments set up in the garage. It was a weird feeling, to ask about someone who hadn't entered his thoughts in years, only to find out the person had already made his exit.

"Did he have a family?" Maria asked.

"A wife and two boys," Frank said. "They're grown. Live in the city."

John nodded, grasping, trying to show he knew something about the man who used to be his best friend. Because when they were kids, John knew everything about Wes. He watched every move he made, imitated everything he did. Parted his hair on the side he did. Dipped fries in mayo instead of ketchup like he did. When Wes came down with mono during senior year, John tried to copy that, too. Moped around in his room for a whole weekend until his dad yelled at him to get the hell up and mow the lawn.

"He was a year away from retirement." Frank took the wrapping paper and crunched it into a ball. "What about you? How long before you retire from this?"

John shrugged, glancing at Maria, since she was always asking him the same thing.

"Punk Button hasn't played since—when, the nineties?" Frank asked.

"Their goodbye tour was in '92. I saw them six times that summer. Got my picture taken with Surge and everything. Maria and I met that year at the show in Minneapolis." John patted her thigh. "It would be hard to let it all go. I've been singing this stuff since—forever." Since right after high school, when The Izz broke up, his mother died, and his father left. When he became Surge.

Maria pulled at a strand of her dark hair and avoided John's eyes. The night he met her, she was wearing a black, spiky wig that made her look like Surge's girlfriend. Maria wore it to most of John's shows those first few years, but now she only pulled it out on Halloween.

Frank pointed at John's empty glass. "Another round? Ha! You must get that all the time."

Later that night, John tried on the skeleton shirt. The bones stretched tight, ready to snap. They sat too high, too close together, like John had taken a jump and everything inside hung in midair.

John was studying for a biology exam the night his father threw the shirt in the yard, along with a milk crate full of albums. *You are* not *going to be one of* them. His father made John bundle everything in black garbage bags and leave it at the curb. In homeroom the next morning, Wes pulled the shirt out of his backpack. Said he'd keep it at his house for him, in the guitar case John already stored there. And Wes had all those records already, so John could listen to them anytime.

Maria paused outside the bedroom door. "You're not really going to wear that anywhere, are you?"

He took it off and folded it back in its box.

Another Round played at Taste of Westmont the following Saturday night. It was a small crowd, but far better than the Daisy shit.

"Yeah, Surge!" someone said between songs. John looked down and saw Frank standing just ten yards away with a slice of pizza. Again, that two-fingered wave.

"What the *fuck?*" John said. Kind of muffled, but still—right into the microphone, with all those kids around. That's the type of thing that could get you banned from a township for life. Luckily, no one seemed to have noticed. But, Jesus, did the guy have nothing better to do than come to these goddamn shows? John used to get women following him from gig to gig—especially before Maria, there'd been quite a few—but never *men.* Look at him, with his big ugly face.

The drum intro pounded, and he felt it flutter in his chest. In his heart. John shook his head, tried to shake off Frank and himself and just *be Surge.* He squirmed his toes in his Chucks.

Felt the pull in the crotch of his black jeans. Took a deep breath and clenched his jaw, feeling it bulge the way it did in those photos of Surge in London. The music ramped up, and he sang.

After the show, he went straight for the Porta John. When he got back, he saw Frank sitting on the edge of the stage, talking and laughing with Mike, Dave, Paul, and Maria. Frank punched Mike on the arm, like old pals.

"Surge! John!" Frank said. "We were thinking of hanging out at the Uptown for a while."

We. Before he could answer, the group started moving in that direction. John followed.

At the bar, Frank pulled him aside. "I have something to ask you." Frank took a deep breath. "I have Wes' old guitar now, and I've been trying to teach myself how to play. I know I'll never be good enough to play on the stage, but I was wondering if I could jam with you sometime? Just to try it out?" The little-boy eagerness was too much.

"I don't know, Frank, I'm really busy with work and practices and shows."

Frank looked away. "Can you just tell me—did Wes use a pick, or not?"

"No." They had fought about it once, but Wes kept dropping them and told John to shut the fuck up about it.

John had only seen Wes twice since high school. The most recent time was about ten years ago, at Butterfield's Pancake House. It was when Maria's mother was sick, and John had gone home after a show with an oily-faced woman named Lisa. She woke him up the next morning asking if he didn't just crave fresh fruit and fresh-squeezed orange juice, and something about the way she said it made him feel like he'd slept on top of a dewy mountain. So the hostess showed them to a table and lo and behold, there was Wes with his fresh-squeezed family. His wife was thin and pretty, and their sons looked helpful, like they would go home and spend the day mowing the lawn and pruning trees. John could feel his face turning red when he introduced Lisa, braless and bulging in her sundress. He went to the men's room halfway through the meal and vomited blueberry pancakes on the floor.

The other time was at John's mother's funeral. Wes had just graduated college and came with his parents, shaking John's hand like he was making a business deal. Wes mentioned his job at the bank and his girlfriend from somewhere out east. They were going to get married next spring and buy a house on the north side. If Wes sent an invitation, it arrived after John got his own apartment. After John's father took off. Before John realized there was no forwarding address.

By the third show of the summer, John didn't think twice when Frank's boyish face—Wes' face—appeared in the crowd. But he did a double-take at the bar afterwards, when he saw that Frank had stuck about fifteen safety pins through his white T-shirt. They made an uneven column down the center of his chest, as if his mother kept using a new pin to attach his lunch money before sending him off to school each day.

Frank saw John staring. "I don't think I'm doing it right. Can you show me how?"

"How to stick a fucking pin through a shirt?" John took a slug of beer and rolled his eyes. John started to wonder if the guy was actually slow.

John almost offered to give his back to the guy, but he didn't want to think about Frank's skin where his had been.

"I still can't find the shirt that matches yours."

"Maybe you just need to fix the ones at the bottom," Maria said. "Here." She leaned across the table and shifted the pins the way she adjusted IVs on her patients.

Frank held the shirt away from his chest for her and smiled when she was done. And that's when John's heart flopped, like skipping a beat on a drum. It had happened to him on stage before, plenty of times, and he'd always thought it was just from excitement. It had never happened when he was just sitting around. He thought of Wes having his heart attack. Goddamn. What were the tell-tale signs? Numbness? Tingling? He made a fist with his left hand under the table and flexed it, as if gearing up to punch Frank in his fucking face.

A few days later, John's cell phone rang while he was at work, loading granola bars into a vending machine at a chiropractic office. Frank.

"You answer this line yourself? I thought you'd have a secretary or something."

It took John a second to realize that Frank had gotten this number off the band website, and that he thought they needed a secretary to book gigs or something. John wasn't even sure Frank knew he worked at Pop's during the week.

"I'm real sorry to bother you," Frank said, "But I'm going through Wes' old albums, and I wondered if you know which Punk Button song was his favorite."

"Are you kidding me?"

"I feel like I should know. But he never told me stuff like that."

John leaned his head against the machine and let it rest there. "'Living the Dream.' That's Maria's favorite, too."

"But not yours."

John paused. "I think 'Another Round' is better." He caught a glimpse of his reflection in the glass door of the machine and saw his father's profile within his own. He straightened his posture, puffed his hair and saw himself morphing into Surge once again.

"I'll have to listen to them both and see," Frank said.

"Great. Let me know what you decide."

John hung up on him and looked back at his reflection. He stood there and studied it for a long time.

That night he dreamed that Wes tied John's hands behind his back and threaded safety pins through his sternum. He kept having to take them out and put them back through to get them straight. They went right through the bone, no blood. He woke up with a tight guitar string thrumming in his chest. He let out a gasp, and Maria stirred beside him. She propped herself up on one elbow and wiped the sweat from his face.

"I'm worried about you," she said. "You're overdoing it with all these shows and the practices during the week. It's taking a toll on you."

"But this is what I *do*. It's who I *am*."

It started the winter after Wes went away to college. The power went out in an ice storm one night when John was tending bar at The Jamba Hut, and John joked that he could feel the surge, the same thing Surge used to say before a concert. John climbed up on a table in front of the dead jukebox and sang punk by candlelight. A dozen people stayed and cheered. He remembered thinking, if only Wes could see me now.

"But maybe you should slow it down. You don't know your parents' health history."

She was being careful. He didn't even know if his father was still alive.

"I'm just worried about you," Maria said. Her voice went higher in pitch, like pulling a slide along the strings of a guitar. "So is Frank."

"Worried about *me*. Is that right. Well, that's just fucking great."

"Hey."

"Sorry. I just—that guy is bugging the hell out of me."

"I've noticed."

John started seeing Frank-Wes everywhere he went. John would sign in at the front desk of an office building to restock the vending machines, and he'd catch a glimpse of him passing at the end of a hall. Or John would be stuck at a traffic light and see Frank-Wes in sunglasses a couple cars back. The guy was pumping gas at the Citgo and bagging groceries at the Jewel. Each time, it sent John's heart pounding.

When he arrived with the band to set up for Heritage Fest, he went up to the information booth and asked if he could switch stages with Another One Bites the Dust. Another Round, Another One . . . close enough, so why not just pull a switcharoo? It was a huge festival, so maybe Frank wouldn't figure it out and John could go through one damn show without that motherfucker grinning up at him. But they said it was too late, the signs all said Another Round was playing on Stage A, and that was the better one anyway. So, John better get up there and set up his equipment because they had a schedule to stick to.

"Another round, this lost and found, feels like drowwwn-ing . . ." John sang.

Frank wore his white safety pin shirt and looked like he'd just trimmed his hair again. He stood near Maria and the band wives, but just a few steps behind, so John couldn't tell if Frank was watching him or Maria. And John could let Maria think he was singing to her when he was really just watching Frank. Making sure he didn't get too close to her.

"The same old song, gone on too long, what the hell went wronnng . . ."

They played for an hour, and then John felt himself sway slightly on the stage. He was lightheaded. He couldn't tell if it was from the beer or the heat or if he was having another fake heart attack. Frank was standing beside Maria now. Almost brushing elbows.

"This next one goes out to Fang," John said. "Right there. You." He pointed. He tipped his head back and sang "Dark Side," a song about the devil.

When the song ended, he turned to the guys behind him and sliced a finger along his neck. He needed to end it early. John waved to the crowd, jumped off the stage and made his way to the parking deck. He sat in his car with the air conditioning cranked until Maria figured out where he was.

"I'm making you an appointment with Dr. Green," she said.

John used to be able to see into the Joneses' house in winter, when the sycamores between the yards had shriveled into claws. From the upstairs bathroom, John could watch Wes in his blue-walled room, tuning his guitar and eating cereal straight from the box by the fistful. Sometimes he had a girl there with him. Usually that blonde one from the drama club, who was cast as the adulteress in *Godspell*. John had a big crush on her, too, and watching Wes with her was almost like being with her himself. They'd start out standing, kissing by the window, where Wes had to curve his spine at a funny angle to reach her mouth. Then they'd move to the bed, where all John could see was the girl's long arms reaching, as if rehearsing her lines with dramatic inflection. One night, he glanced down and saw Frank's face staring back at him from the basement window.

He went home after the doctor appointment and lay down on the couch. His diagnosis was *stress*. Some people get a heart problem from high-pressure jobs at big-time banks, but John gets it from *playing music.* Music is supposed to relieve stress, but oh no, not for John. Leave it to him to be the medical freak.

Maria wanted him to cancel a few upcoming gigs, but he said no. He couldn't, especially since they were playing Ribfest. He agreed to at least scale things back—no encores and not a lot of jumping around on the stage in the heat.

He was just starting to drift off to sleep when his phone rang.

"I do think 'Living the Dream' is the better song," the voice said.

"You've given it some thought, have you?"

"Yes, I've listened to every song on every album, and I can see why you narrowed it down to those two, but—"

"You're killing me."

"I know, I kind of thought I'd end up agreeing with you on this."

"I mean, you're actually *killing* me."

Frank called several times a week now, almost always with a question. John stopped answering the phone when he saw Frank's number come up, and just let it all go to voicemail. Listening to the messages was like being interviewed for *The Chord*. What was Wes' favorite TV show? Did he actually fail biology, or was that their parents being dramatic? Did he get that drama club girl pregnant, or was that a rumor? Was he really going to join the army after high school if he didn't get into a good college? Was Wes a jerk to everyone, or just his brother?

One day John took the call. "So, what's the deal, man?" he asked. "You're living at your parents' house again. You still making robots and shit in the basement, too, like old times?"

Silence.

"Why do you keep coming to the shows?" John asked.

"They're fun."

"For me."

"Guess I wanted to get to know my brother through you. Who he was before the world changed him."

Memories glinted in the distance—kids jeering at Frank in the halls at school. A science fair ribbon pinned on his robot. The guys cutting holes into his shorts during gym class.

"So, thank you," Frank said. "Wes' wife won't speak to me. I think they were about to get a divorce or something when he died, and she doesn't want to keep in touch. His sons don't return my calls."

"Well. You're welcome."

John showed up hours early the day they played Ribfest. He parked over at The Office Bar, figuring that's where they'd end up after the show, and got himself a full rack of ribs for free from one of the tents. It was like eating straight from the cash cow. People herded past while he ate. It was going to be a great show—their biggest by far. Another Round might never get that national tour, but this was pretty close.

Frank had asked, "Did Wes ever want to play music full-time, like you do?"

John thought for a minute. "Always. Since the day he was born."

"He said you couldn't sing."

"I *couldn't sing* because that was his rule."

That night it took him a while to find Maria in the crowd. She usually stood to the left of the stage, but tonight she was dead center. He expected to see Frank beside or behind her, but no. John felt a little surge in his chest, like getting away with a minor theft.

John searched the faces. So many people; Frank could be any-where. After "Living the Dream," he cupped his hands around his eyes and scanned the crowd. There were a few people with similar haircuts, but different builds. Some with the same nervous demeanor, but none of the same features. The show ended. No Frank. And John had spent his entire Ribfest debut looking for the guy.

He and Maria and the rest of the gang closed down The Office Bar afterward. Mike and Maria both asked about Frank, as if John would have any idea where he was. John kept watching the door, waiting for Frank to sidle in at any moment, but the damn guy never showed.

He didn't come next weekend, either, when they played a show in Berwyn.

John started watching for him to appear behind the dumpster outside the apartment, in the stairwell at work, under a tree at Mike's house when he showed up for practice. If he looked hard enough, the leaves formed the shape of his face.

"Something must be *wrong*, John," Maria said. "You need to call him."

"It's not wrong. It's *normal*. No grown man follows a tribute band like some kind of sad groupie."

But John did call, for Wes' sake. He found the most recent message from Frank and hit redial. It went straight to voicemail, and John left a recording that embarrassed him when he thought of it.

"Frank? You all right?"

A few days later John finished up work early and decided to swing by the old neighborhood. He'd never been back, not once in all these years, but he knew right where to turn. He pulled onto Jamison Court, rounded a grove of sycamores, and there it was: John's house. Someone had painted it blue, but they couldn't fool him. It was still yellow underneath.

And to its left, Wes' old house. Frank's house. Still white with black shutters, but a little dirty these days. Did it look like Frank still lived there? What would Frank still living there look like?

John realized he didn't know anything about the guy, what kind of car he drove, if he'd found a job, or what he'd done in Kansas City or St. Louis or wherever the hell he'd been living before. Frank had said he'd only be in town for a while, but you'd think he'd have the courtesy to say goodbye before he left.

John felt an overwhelming desire to feel the sidewalk under his feet. He parked at the curb a few houses down and pulled some paperwork out of the glove box. There was a U.S. Postal Service mailbox at the corner; he'd pretend he was mailing something, just in case someone was watching. He counted his steps, the way he used to do as a kid, pacing himself to miss the cracks. Forty-two strides to the mailbox. He stood there for a while, pretending to read the pickup times. Noon and five o'clock, good, yes. His old house watched him. He couldn't believe they painted it *blue*. His mother wouldn't have liked it.

Commercials flashed on a TV screen, from the same corner where John's parents had kept their set. Where his mother watched soaps and his father watched the news. And sometimes the two of them would watch a movie together, his father in the recliner and his mother with a magazine on her lap, and John would walk in and see them there and think, what a shitty existence.

A woman shifted now in the arm chair by the picture window, and he was fifteen again. John could almost see the sad slope of his mother's profile, the complacent curve of her shoulders. He wanted to rap on the glass and warn her. She would find out about the cancer in a few years, and she'd be dead in two months. His father would not be able to handle it. He wanted to fix her a cup of tea. He wanted his father to appear and shake his hand, man to man, but he wasn't home.

It was three o'clock, the time John and Wes and Frank would have just been walking back from school if this were forty years ago. The basement was dark, but a light shone in an upstairs window. Wes' old room. He was moving around in there, shaking crumbs from a chip bag directly into his mouth. It was Frank, of course, not Wes. Frank brushed the dust from his shirt. It was a dark one. Maybe it was the skeleton shirt. Maybe he'd finally found it.

And maybe Frank *had* said goodbye, and John just hadn't heard it. Maybe Frank had learned enough about Wes and he'd moved on now, as people do.

But if John and Frank were friends, John thought they might put on the matching shirts and pose for a picture, just for the hell of it. Maybe they'd sit and have a beer or two. John would ask where Frank has been, and Frank wouldn't turn red for once. He'd say he's been busy helping his parents with some projects, or maybe now he was working weekends someplace. Maybe they'd bring out the guitars, and Frank might surprise him with how well he plays.

I can't stay too long, John would say. He had to get home to Maria, home to his life.

What the hell went wronnng . . .

He almost expected an answer, but the people who could offer one were gone.

Have another round, Frank would say, just to hear John groan. *For old time's sake*. As if they'd shared old times. Frank would twist off the cap with the edge of his shirt—all those bones jangling—and hand it over, and they'd ask each other about their childhoods and pretending to be grown men and what it was like to look up to people who weren't there. John and Frank were the survivors; all they had to do was keep living, keep doing what they did—and it didn't even matter what that was anymore.

After a while, John would head back to the car and he'd notice that when he isn't thinking about Surge, the gait he assumes is his father's. It belongs to John, too, now, this manner of leaning hard on the balls of his feet and hitching his left hip ever so slightly, and he gives himself over to it as he walks, feeling the rhythm of his stride as it taps at the core of his being, like bass beating steady in his heart.

A+ Electric

was sitting on the kitchen counter, eating pickles from the jar, when the front door clicked open. I figured the latch was busted again, but in walked our neighbor man and two kids younger than me wearing men's polo shirts. All three of them held rolled-up sleeping bags like drums.

"We been playing hide and seek," the man said. "So far, we're winning." He crouched against the refrigerator and told the kids to sit by the stove. I remembered seeing them once before—two blurs running around the house down the block on their weekend with their dad.

The man pulled a grease-spotted bag out of his backpack and let me dig for the biggest piece of fried chicken. Nobody ever let me have the biggest piece of fried chicken. I sat on the open dishwasher door to eat it while I studied the man. He looked different without his hands on a lawnmower.

I was still working on the skin when Mom came out of her room, her hair matted from her afternoon nap. She looked from the kids to the man and said, "You meant today?"

He offered her the bag, and she took a drumstick.

"Get down," he said, and she hunched beside the kids. Together, they looked like a hedgerow. I wanted to brush their hair, even the boy's. He was the youngest.

The man reached into his backpack again and pulled out a pair of binoculars. He crawled over to the sink and crept up until he could just see out the window. It was already dark out. His reflection stared back like a peeper. When he twisted the eye-pieces, his fingers made the black plastic shiny.

"Ready or not, here I come," he said, setting the binoculars on the counter. The front door clicked again, and he was gone.

We all sat for a moment more, as if waiting out the final gust of a tornado. Then Mom collected the chicken bones in a napkin, moving through the kitchen like a hunchback so she wouldn't be seen from outside. But the kids watched her. She patted their heads and touched her own, and I wondered if they were our kids now.

A rumble began in the distance. The neighbor man's old truck with the broken muffler. It thundered up our driveway and continued into the backyard, snapping tree branches like a storm. The front door clicked again. "Bring a flashlight," he said.

We ran out and around the house, following the beam of Mom's Maglite. The kids' hair looked like spider webs in the glow. The man wrenched the lid off a paint can and used broad brush-strokes to cover the A+ ELECTRIC logo on the side of the truck. He stepped back and then ran at the truck again with the brush, jumping from the bed to the roof and down again until the whole thing was dripping black like part of the night.

"To us," he said, pulling a flask from his pocket and tapping it against the Maglite. "Let them tell me I can't take care of my kids."

The adults took the flask to the kitchen, and I took the boy and girl upstairs to hide in my room. I squirted toothpaste onto their fingers so they could rub it on their teeth. I poured them mugs of water. I spread their sleeping bags beside my bed, tucked them in and brushed their hair, counting the strokes and wondering how high I'd get before someone found us and took them away from me.

Step Off at Ten

My husband didn't want me at the Saint Patrick's Day parade.

"It's going to be colder than they thought," he said early that morning. "Maybe you should keep Gwen home."

Ed spoke into his dresser drawer, trying to sound casual. He pulled out a brown sock and a gray sock and held them against each other, sizing them up like women.

"We'll be fine," I said.

"I don't know where I am in the lineup." He raised his eyebrows. "You might end up waiting a long time, and you know how hard it can be to watch Gwen in a crowd."

The words took on authority. He was, after all, the Grundy village trustee in charge of public health and safety, the champion of safety reform ever since the granary explosion killed three of his employees four years ago.

Gwen had been talking about the parade all week, how she'd get to see her dad drive the big grain truck down the middle of Main Street. He knew she'd be disappointed if she didn't get to go.

He found two matching socks and sat on the edge of our bed to put them on. He looked like an actor in a movie, a man in a hotel room, a man who knew a woman was watching him get dressed.

Her name was Melissa. She was back in his life. I knew it.

There had been other signs. He'd started keeping his phone in his pocket instead of putting it on the kitchen counter when he got home from work. I'd find him texting at odd hours. Work, he'd say, fighting a smile. Plus, I couldn't find two of the shirts I'd gotten him for Christmas.

And the hardest thing: He seemed happier.

Whether Melissa was going to ride in the truck alongside him or meet him for lunch afterward, I felt pretty sure she would be there and he didn't want me to see.

"Don't worry," I said. "We'll stay home." I put my boots back on their shelf in the closet so he'd believe me. I was wearing an old bra, and the wire creaked when I lifted my arms. It sounded like a rope swing ready to snap and send me flying.

He put on his Grundy Granary work coat, the one with the "Go with the grain!" slogan arcing across the back. He collected his wallet and keys and left early, before Gwen got up, saying the town was buying doughnuts and coffee for everyone in the parade. He promised to pick up corned beef for supper on his way home.

Ed and I had promised each other what we were supposed to, that we'd do better than our parents. In a lot of ways, we had. Ed told his friends I was a good mother. He bought me pendants and earrings on Mother's Day. When I held them up to my face, I could see gratitude in his eyes, and I was glad that even if I wasn't enough for him, I was enough for Gwen. But I could also see this was his way of apologizing, and he thought that was enough for me.

I made Gwen green pancakes, and I made her put on two sweaters. When we got in the car, the radio announcer warned of strong winds and a wintry mix. I told Gwen to sit back and buckle up, and she did. Ed usually had to ask her two or three times to do something, but not me.

"Do you think it's a phase?" he asked me last week. "That she'll listen to us better when she starts kindergarten?"

I told him yes. I didn't tell him she was only going through this phase with him. She looked so much like him—the same dark hair, dark eyes and trumpet of a nose, those furrows squirming in her forehead like squid. I used to worry he'd win her over with his jokes and treats and they'd gang up on me. I used to dream about it, the two of them standing on top of a cliff, watching me try to climb my way up to them. Now I was glad to see the frustration in his brow, glad to hear it twisting his words. Drink your milk. Drink your *milk*. *GWEN*do*lyn*. Mink. Your. Drilk.

The frozen Illinois River stretched like a marriage along the right-hand side of the road. I told Gwen to look for bald eagles, and she counted every spec of white litter up to forty and then started over. The first beads of sleet pinged the windshield just as we began the climb along the bluffs. When I looked in the rearview mirror, all I saw was Gwen's doll on the shelf above the backseat, its face reflected in the window like Ophelia under water. The fluttering of its open-shut eyes made me think of sex.

"Stay home if at all possible," the radio announcer said. Even he was on Ed's side.

It was just a parade. I had every right to be there. The flyers had been up all over town for weeks, urging me to come. Get lucky at the first event of the year! Parade steps off at ten! Each exclamation point was dotted with a shamrock. Still, it made me nervous, showing up like this. Like I was barging into a village board meeting or Ed's office unannounced. At what point had things shifted enough to make me feel like the outsider? I blinked and held my eyes open wide, watching the double yellow line zip along the road through the blustery haze.

The grain dust explosion had happened around two o'clock on a Wednesday afternoon. People heard it for miles around, like a meteor slamming into the river. I would have been behind the library circulation desk, but I was home sick with my pregnancy, clutching my stomach as I watched the news alone on the couch. There's the river. There's the granary. There's the guts of the four silos, their concrete roofs blown off and grain scattered everywhere like sand around the sea caves of what was left. Rubble and rebar formed a jungle around it all, as if this had happened slowly over decades, rather than in the instant it takes for a spark to ignite grain dust.

It was a full hour before I found out I wasn't a widow, that I wasn't going to have to raise the baby on my own. Ed wasn't even injured.

No one knew the exact cause of the explosion, but everyone knew the effect. News crews came from all over. Ed became a celebrity spokesperson.

"We'll do whatever it takes to restore safety to this plant and to rebuild what we lost," he said, looking straight into the camera.

The main contact at the construction company doing the rebuilding was Melissa. She was new to the area and had done a couple of big projects in Peoria. Ed worked with her for two years, and together they delivered status updates to his employees and the *Grundy Gazette*. He assured everyone that safety was their top priority. They were working tirelessly to make everything right. They were taking every precaution to ensure nothing like this ever happened again. It made me think of condoms.

When the tire began to slide on the sleet, it felt like a boat breaking free from shore. It almost felt like relief. They say you're supposed to turn the wheel into the spin, but I always forget what that means. I tried everything and nothing worked, especially not the brakes, and the two-lane road seemed too narrow, and then impossibly wide, like the impact I knew was coming never would, but I hoped it would because if it didn't, it would mean we were flying like eagles off the cliff, off the planet, off—and I would never get to see the parade or Gwen or what Ed didn't want me to see.

I saw the sleet, the shaking of the woods and the slam of the tree trunk before it happened. It's the same sensation you get when you're falling asleep in front of the TV and the voices enter your mind before you hear them so it seems you're the one thinking up the dialogue.

There was a second impact, but much softer and from behind. A slam against my headrest. Then silence. My god, I've killed my daughter. Didn't I tell her to buckle herself in? Did she say she did, when she didn't? That would be worse than just disobeying, like she did with Ed. Oh god, what would I tell Ed? I was supposed to be home.

I was already turning, feeling behind the seat, brushing my palm against a cheek, running my fingers through hair before I realized that the cheek was too cold, too hard, too small, and the hair too plasticky to belong to anyone but the doll. The doll, whose name Gwen changed so often that she didn't really have one.

"Anna!" she screamed.

"What?" I said, and I looked at Gwen, buckled in her car seat, like she was someone else's child—or really, not a child at all.

She pointed and I understood that today, Anna was the doll's name, too.

"She's *fine*," I said, meaning the doll as well as Gwen and even the car, but not so much myself. Gwen hugged Anna to her chest and we all looked at how close we'd come—the drop-off inches away, nothing but a birch between us and the frozen river.

I drove off without looking at the damage. I imagined pulling into the library lot and letting people see what kind of wreck the safety trustee let his wife drive. When we got downtown, I parked on a side street and walked around the car. I was surprised—it wasn't too bad. Certainly good enough to carry Gwen and me and all our clothes to my sister's in Nebraska, if it came to that.

It was still windy and frigid, but the sleet had stopped. I snapped the top of Gwen's coat and pulled the flaps of her cap over her ears. We blew puffs of our breath together to make a cloud and walked toward the people gathering along the two blocks of shops and eateries. The weather had kept a lot of people home, but there were enough to clap and cheer. Paper rainbows and plastic pots of gold decorated the windows. Green banners and shamrocks hung from the light poles, and Irish folksongs played over the loudspeakers. Sirens whined under the melody—probably an accident on the interstate. Behind the village bank, the granary loomed with its big, secret silos and steel-ladder backbones.

Melissa would be easy to spot; she'd appeared in some of the *Gazette* articles with Ed, and I'd studied them for hours. She was pretty enough, but her face looked like it had been compressed in a vise. The bridge of her nose was a pencil. I'd never officially met her, unless you count the time she pulled into the granary parking lot at nine o'clock at night and dropped Ed off at his car next to mine, where I'd been sitting since sunset, with Gwen sleeping in the back.

"Thanks for bringing him back *safely*!" I shouted out my window as she pulled away.

"This ends today," I told Ed. And it had. He assured me, and I believed him for a while.

"Let's walk to the end of the block," I told Gwen now. I'd forgotten my gloves, but Gwen's mittened hand provided some warmth as I searched the crowd, avoiding the eyes of people I knew. I tried to look casual, like I hadn't just rammed my car into a tree and wasn't on a mission to find my husband's lover. If I could prove to myself that something was going on, I'd know what to do, I was sure. But until then, all I had was a couple of missing shirts and a husband who wanted to keep me home where I'd be safe.

Something occurred to me: there was no guarantee it was Melissa this time. Maybe there was some new secretary or accountant or waitress at the sandwich shop he liked. As we walked, I stared into the face of every woman I passed. It could be anyone.

This one with the black hair and leather boots. The one beside her in a long puffy coat. I considered the blonde a few feet away, a big sugar cookie of a woman I remembered from the library because she checked out five romance novels at a time.

When we got near the end of the block, I stopped so Gwen and I could stay hidden in the crowd. Around the corner on First Street, the procession waited for the cue to move forward. I didn't see the grain truck, just a troop of Boy Scouts holding a banner, a van with the name of a church on the side, and a fire truck with two firefighters on top. The rest of the lineup disappeared behind the Good Family Insurance building. I'd lost track of time, but it must have been after ten. I turned, looking for the street clock, and there she was, right on the curb. Pencil nose. Narrow face. She was alone, bending her knees and rocking back on the heels of her purple snow boots. She wore dark jeans and a bulky coat. A Grundy Granary work coat. It was just like Ed's, and I thought it might *be* Ed's, but this one looked new. She wore a pink-ribbon pin for breast cancer up near the collar.

"Here's the perfect spot," I said to Gwen. I picked her up, rested her on my hip and pushed through the crowd until we were standing next to Melissa. "Now we'll be able to see your dad in full view."

When Melissa saw us, she froze as if the cold had finally overcome her.

"Are you the official photographer?" I asked, pointing to her camera.

Melissa cleared her throat. "I'm supposed to get a picture of the truck going by."

"That'll be great publicity," I said cheerily. "Showing that the company is really *involved* in the community."

Melissa blinked, and her eyes darted up and down the street. The tufts of dark hair poking out around her hat were streaked with bleach-blond highlights.

"Your dad is going to be so happy to see you here," I said, bouncing Gwen on my hip the way I used to when she was a baby. She started to struggle, and I set her down next to me.

"What do you do for them?" I asked. "I mean, I know what you do for *Ed*, but are you actually employed at the granary? Or did he just buy you a coat?"

Melissa stepped out into the street and found a spot a few feet away. I followed her. "Seriously," I said. "I need to know. Do you work there now?"

Her eyes met mine, and something shifted.

"I'm the new office manager," she said.

I didn't think they'd ever had an office manager before. "When did you start?" I asked.

"About a month ago."

"Do you want to marry him?" I asked.

Melissa didn't say anything for some time.

"He says he wants to marry me," she finally said.

I hadn't considered that. I felt like we were talking about someone else, an actor in some movie that would be celebrated for its high drama. I thought of the man who worked the children's circulation desk at the library and got to see his sons every other weekend.

Melissa busied herself by pressing buttons on her camera. "I wonder what's holding them up," she said, craning her neck. "I just need this *one photo*."

I watched her, guessing her age. She looked young, but it might have been because of the closeness of her eyes, as if she needed more time to spread out, but maybe this was all there was to her. I was the one falling out of my senses, my skin, my life, but she was tightly contained.

A scream interrupted my thoughts. A siren. I somehow heard the echo first—I looked left, where the wail reverberated off the storefronts, and then right, where the fire truck was lit like an arcade, red lights spinning and headlights flashing. The parade was starting. The Boy Scouts led the procession around the corner onto Main Street. Their parents waved and shouted names. Billy! Jason! Most of the boys waved back, stepping out of formation, smiling and looking around. But the boy holding the banner in front stayed focused on his steps, marching, one, two, three, four, since he had the most important job of the day, leading the entire parade down the middle of the street where you weren't normally allowed to walk.

I took Gwen's hand and slipped behind Melissa, through the crowd and around the corner to where the procession was backed up. My eyes darted along the lineup, past the church van, the VFW float, the Harley Davidson Club, the Kiwanis Club, the Rotary Club—and landed on the grain truck with its giant red box and hoist. I waited until the truck turned onto Main Street and scooped up Gwen and rushed out to meet it. I matched my pace to the truck and ambled along just behind the driver's side door. Ed didn't see us right away. He was busy throwing fistfuls of candy into the crowd. He had his window all the way down with the heat blasting. When Gwen called to him, he jumped in his seat like he'd been caught with his hand down Melissa's pants instead of in the candy.

"What's wrong? Did something happen?" he asked.

"No," I said. "We just wanted to show our support for you."

"Well, come around and get inside where it's warm."

"I'd rather walk." I smiled and waved to the crowd, no longer wanting to avoid the eyes of people I knew. I called out to a family of five that I recognized from the library. Ed watched me in the side mirror.

"Here, we'll throw the candy," I said, grabbing the bag. "You should keep your hands at ten and two."

Ed gripped the wheel, his arms fully extended like he was bracing for impact.

"Chocolate coins, very fancy," I said, handing one to Gwen and throwing fistfuls into the crowd. I waved when I spotted Gwen's pediatrician and again when we passed the grocery store clerk who always handed the receipt to Gwen. I even waved to the sugar-cookie woman. They had no idea that this was goodbye.

We could see Melissa now—she was up on the left. She stepped into the street with her camera raised, and then lowered it when she saw me.

"Looks like you're out of giveaways," I said to Ed, shaking the empty bag and tossing it up at him. "Oh wait—" I wrenched my wedding ring off the hand supporting Gwen and held it out for Ed to see. "Here's one more."

As we passed Melissa, I threw as hard as I could. I caught a glimpse of gold as the ring bounced in the gutter beside her. I focused on my steps and this lucky road that would lead me back to my dented car, the icy bluffs, and all the wondrous risks that lay west beyond the river.

Intensify the Feeling

Ruby and her daughter hadn't eaten dinner together in thirteen years. Now it was getting late—dark for hours already—and they were hungry, but they let the bags of burritos and chocolate cake sit untouched on the counter like a dare. Beth wanted to wait until her friend from work came.

"She said to start without her, but she just left the office," Beth said, holding up her phone. "She'll be here in ten minutes."

Not enough time to eat without seeming rude, or to talk about anything real. Beth had already pushed aside Ruby's questions about her broken leg and her broken engagement, saying only that the steps had been icy and it's for the best. So they sat with the cast stretched between them like the weekend ahead—a shell over everything that needed healing.

"You'll like Eva," Beth said.

"You've said that." Ruby regretted her tone and added, "I'm sure I will." It's true, she'd like the distraction as much as Beth. Ruby preferred small talk, just as Beth preferred to evade attention when she needed it most.

"But don't forget—I'm here to take *care* of you," Ruby had said when she'd arrived an hour ago, saying the words for herself as much as for Beth. It's what mothers did for their children, even after they were grown. Still, Beth had only asked for burritos because Ruby liked them, and cake to commemorate her brother's upcoming birthday. It would have been his fortieth.

"Is your dad coming up to see you?" Ruby asked.

Beth nodded. "Monday. He insisted on taking the whole week off."

Of course he did. It was just like Chuck to let Ruby have the first shot at this and then swoop in like a red pen, correcting it all and pulling Beth closer in the process. But Beth and Chuck had always been close, even before everything went to hell.

Beth sat on the only real chair in the place—a simple brown recliner Ruby had bought her when she moved into her first apartment fifteen years ago. Ruby sat on a garage-sale footstool, its fabric frayed and speckled with what looked to be candle wax. Most of the other furniture wasn't furniture at all, but milk crates packed with books and stacked like blocks, with lamps and empty glasses teetering on top.

"Maybe tomorrow I'll get you a couch," Ruby said. "And a bookshelf. Those can be your Christmas gifts." She'd sent a box of chocolates three weeks ago for the holidays, along with the offer to order something off the wedding registry, if Beth had one yet. She hadn't responded.

Beth nodded hesitantly, and then stopped herself. "That's okay," she said, as if Ruby had just spilled something on the mottled carpet. Beth's dark eyes brimmed with Chuck's earnestness—a look that reminded Ruby of shame.

"Had you planned to get a new place after the wedding, or move in with Tyson?" she asked, saying the name with uncertainty.

"I don't know," Beth said. She pulled her hair back from her face, and her arm fat wobbled under the sleeves of her too-small White Sox sweatshirt.

It now seemed both impossible and fortunate that Ruby had never met Tyson. She'd only seen a couple old photos of him—one with his arm around Beth at a Blackhawks game, and one of him holding a plate of lobster, looking bewildered. Ruby had hoped she might find some recent pictures in the apartment, but the place was devoid of personal touches. The only things clinging to the refrigerator door were takeout menus and utility bills. And the only wall decoration was a State Farm calendar still open to December, where Beth had drawn a diagonal line through every day. She would have liked to think Beth had already been living with Tyson, that she'd rarely slept in this sterile environment, but she was afraid that wasn't the case.

"Well, you must have had some idea of where you'd live." Ruby felt the heat rising in her cheeks. She'd told herself she wasn't going to get impatient this time, that she would even try to joke around with Beth the way she used to with her son, Noah, but so far her efforts weren't going so well.

Beth picked lint off her pink sweatpants, and for a moment Ruby thought she might be crying. But then she lifted her face—a few degrees too high—and said, "He bought us a house in the suburbs."

Ruby wondered for the first time if Beth had been the one to call off the wedding.

"But he also owns a condo here in the city," Beth added. "We weren't sure which one we were going to rent out."

"He sounds like a successful man."

Like someone Ruby would have hated. Some overgrown kid with rich parents. Or some older man with ex-wives in other states.

"I know what you're thinking," Beth said.

Ruby shook her head, shook away the thought that her daughter wasn't good enough for a man she didn't even know.

Beth's work friend, Eva, was much older than Ruby had imagined— possibly older than Ruby herself. Pearl-studded combs held her wavy gray hair away from her face, revealing thick jaw muscles that suggested a lifetime of tooth grinding. A gold cross gleamed at her throat like a dog tag. The whole effect was that of a cocker spaniel. She gave Ruby a terse smile and a firm handshake, but she hugged Beth warmly, a few seconds longer than reasonable, and whispered something in her ear. Beth nodded, and Eva patted her arm.

"Something to drink?" Eva asked, whirling around to face Ruby, who was still standing awkwardly in the middle of the room.

"We're having Mexican—I should have made a pitcher of margaritas," Ruby said, forcing a laugh.

"Beth couldn't have had any," Eva said. "Not with all the pain medicine she's taking."

"Well, no, of course not." Ruby frowned. She followed Eva into the kitchen and watched as she pulled three glasses from the cabinet and filled them from the tap. Her black blazer gave every movement an official, persuasive air that made Ruby think the woman probably worked in the marketing department.

Ruby couldn't think of anything to say, so she went back for the burritos and rolled them out onto a blue plate she found in the dish drainer. She scanned the countertops and paused. "You don't have a microwave?" she asked.

"It broke," Beth said.

"That's okay," Eva said. She wrapped her hands around the water glasses like a pool ball triangle and carried them to the next room.

Ruby searched the cabinets and found more plates. Four forks stood in a chipped Santa mug—the kind you buy at the drugstore with a bag of cheap hard candy inside. All the spoons and knives lay scattered in the sink, bearing evidence of what looked to be a diet of pudding and peanut butter. Ruby grabbed the mug and sat it next to Beth, but no one used them. Ruby ate quickly, conscious of the way she towered over Eva, who sat cross-legged on the floor and explained, in great detail, the status of a dreadful-sounding project that required telemarketing.

When Eva finished talking, Beth spoke up. "So, I had a real reason for wanting you two to meet." She looked from Eva to Ruby and back. "You have something in common."

Ruby tried to look hopeful, but instead felt herself turning into a smiley-face pancake. Age was the only thing Ruby could possibly have in common with this woman. What else could it be? They use the same moisturizer? They both drink their coffee black? Even that seemed impossible; Eva was undoubtedly a cream-and-three-sugars type of person.

"I'll just be blunt," Beth said, though she'd never been blunt about a thing in her life. "You both had a child who died by suicide."

Ruby's smile fell off her face. She wanted to walk out the door, say it was a mistake to be here, that clearly Beth was in good hands with Eva, and maybe she'd come back when Beth's leg healed so they could finally go on one of those walking architecture tours they'd talked about for years.

And then Ruby saw something: Eva already knew. Beth had talked about it with her. Probably often. Probably with that exact wording. It was the preferred way to say it these days, but it sounded too rhymey—like a novel marketed to women. *Died*, by Sue Aside. Ruby had grown up with the verb "commit." That's how she and Chuck used to talk about Noah; they'd said he committed suicide, as if it involved paperwork and signatures. Chuck had used the word in other ways, too, especially in the months leading to the divorce—like when he said he ought to have Ruby committed. And that he was the only one who was committed to the marriage. In the end, he was right.

Eva was the first to speak. "My daughter. It will be two years in March."

"I'm sorry," Ruby said. "How old?"

"Sixteen. But she was young for her age, if you know what I mean. She didn't know things would get better."

"I always felt like Noah was old for his age," Ruby said. "That he should have known better."

"You shouldn't say that," Beth said. She'd barely touched her burrito. It lay limp on her plate, a miniature cast.

"I just mean—he was a smart kid," Ruby said. She turned to Eva. "I'm sure your daughter was, too. What was her name?"

"Elizabeth," Eva said.

Ruby looked at Beth, and back at Eva. "I see."

"It's been longer for you," Eva said. "Does it get better? The pain?"

"Twenty-three years. And no."

"Really?" Beth said.

Ruby wasn't sure what to make of the hope she detected in Beth's voice. "Well, everybody's grieving process is different," Ruby said, putting a hand to the base of her neck, where her short, dyed-red hair was starting to curl. She needed a trim, and she hated herself for thinking it right then.

"Yes, everybody's different," Eva said, and for a moment Ruby felt somehow vindicated. But then Eva pushed herself up from the floor and passed out thick slices of chocolate cake, pausing to ask Beth if she needed anything, and it became clear Eva meant Ruby was the one who was different. But only Ruby knew how different she really was. She and Eva didn't even have the one thing in common Beth thought they did. Ruby had repeated the lie for years, but the truth remained: Noah hadn't actually committed suicide.

Late that night, Ruby lay awake in Beth's twin-size bed—Beth had insisted on the arrangement, claiming she'd sleep better on the recliner—watching headlights pan across the plain white walls. Tires squealed up the block on Halsted, bass thumped upstairs with urgency, and every few minutes a sliding glass door slammed open and shut for balcony smokers at a party next door.

Ruby's niece, Lectra, the only person Beth knew in Chicago when she moved here, had lived in a building nearby until she got raped, dropped out of UIC, and moved back to Crestfall. There'd been some discussion, then, about whether it was safe for Beth to stay here—anywhere in the city at all—with Chuck voicing the most concern, as he'd only been to Chicago a few times and was afraid of all things unfamiliar.

"I don't think I need to worry," Beth had said simply.

Ruby and Chuck had let it go at that, each daring the other to put their foot down, neither one wanting to be the bad guy. It was a game they'd played ever since Noah died, especially since the divorce—who could be more protective, but not too protective, of their only surviving child.

They used to talk a lot about the city and its dangers at Life Lines, back when Ruby was involved with the group. They'd meet in the church basement on Wednesday nights for seminars with names like City Mouse, Saintly Mouse; Working God into Work; and The Magnificent Lifestyle: Shop and Dine Your Way to Heaven. Chuck would make a pamphlet based on each seminar, and the Evangelism Committee would drive to the city one Saturday a month to hand out copies on Michigan Avenue. The head of the committee, Ruby realized now, reminded her of Eva—or vice versa. They had the same self-assured faith that Ruby once envied.

Noah and Beth were in grade school when Ruby started teaching the Life Lines teen abstinence workshops for high-schoolers. Boys on one side of the room, girls on the other. The curriculum and materials were provided for her—all she had to do was read the PowerPoint and lead the role-playing exercises.

Pretend you're on a date, and things start getting serious. How far is too far?

Ruby called on an equal number of boys and girls. No tongue, someone would suggest in a voice just above a whisper.

No touching, someone else would say, their face turning red. Someone would suggest touching is okay, but not under clothes, and everyone would turn and stare at them. Then Ruby would read the correct answer from the course materials: *Anything you do with your date is okay, as long as you both stay seated and clothed, with your feet flat on the floor.*

The students would consider this, wondering if it had to be both feet, imagining what could happen if one lifted off the ground. They didn't know the half of it. And the presentation's author didn't know just how much two seated people could do, given the flexibility of the human body.

Pretend things do go too far. How will you stop?

Tell your date you're waiting for marriage, someone would suggest. Stand up and leave, someone else would say. Or hold hands and pray about it.

Pretend you're home alone, and you have impure thoughts. How can you resist giving in to self-pleasure?

Go for a walk. Make a sandwich. Do something that keeps your hands and mind busy, like building a model airplane.

Now pretend it's a weekday and your teenage son doesn't come down for breakfast, so you go to his room and find him hanging by his neck in the closet. How will you tell your family? Your pastor? Your students?

Ruby went to the basement early the next morning to start a load of Beth's laundry. It was Saturday, and she was afraid the machines would fill up fast. Plus, she needed something to do.

"You've done so much already!" Beth said, as if Ruby had been there for a week instead of a night. "You don't have to wash my clothes, too."

"Well, *you* can't do it," Ruby said. And if she didn't, Eva would.

When she went down to transfer the clothes into the dryer, Eva was standing in the middle of the room as if Ruby had conjured her up, and for a moment Ruby thought the woman had, in fact, come to finish the job. Ruby wondered how Eva knew she was doing laundry, but then she remembered Beth had been glued to her phone all morning—obviously, the two had been texting. Ruby imagined a long string of pitying questions from Eva about Beth's leg and how she'd slept and how things were going with her mom.

"Good morning," Eva said with sunshine in her voice. The same combs swept up her hair, but she wore a baggy sweatshirt, jeans, and furry brown boots that clung to her shins like puppies.

"I didn't mean to startle you," Eva said. "But I need to talk to you, and I wasn't sure how else to find you without Beth knowing."

Ruby felt like she was about to be reprimanded. "You found me," she said. "How'd you get in?" she asked, thinking of the secure building entrance, last night's ordeal of making sure she had Beth's keys before going to get the burritos.

"I have Beth's spares."

Of course.

Eva clasped her hands around her purse strap in a way that made her look like a tourist visiting the city for the first time.

"Beth has been going through a tough time," Eva said.

"I know that," Ruby said.

The compassion in Eva's eyes was so intense, her eyebrows angled so severely with concern, that Ruby couldn't look at her anymore. It was like watching someone pray with their eyes closed and their hands in the air, swaying. She turned and began pulling wet laundry into Beth's cracked laundry basket.

"She didn't slip on the ice," Eva said.

"No?" Ruby pulled out two pairs of underwear so tattered, they dangled from their elastic waistbands like bluegill. She tossed them into the garbage can.

"She stepped out into traffic," Eva said. "On purpose."

Ruby reached back into the washing machine and pulled out a couple of faded sweatshirts. The drawstring had come out of one of the hoodies. Ruby sighed, balled it up, and put it in her pocket.

"Did you hear me?" Eva came closer.

"How could you know it was on purpose?"

"Because I was with her when it happened." Eva gestured to the air next to her. "We were working late, and by the time we left it was sleeting and she—she said she wasn't afraid of dying anymore. She was right there beside me and then all of a sudden she wasn't."

"You're telling me she walked into the road?" It seemed absurd.

"Yes. We got to an intersection and we were supposed to keep going straight for another few blocks, but she veered off the curb to the left, right in front of a delivery truck that was turning. He swerved and only hit her leg, but the impact knocked her back onto the sidewalk. She got a concussion and scraped up her arms pretty badly."

"A concussion."

"That's why they kept her overnight."

Ruby nodded. It still hurt to know Beth hadn't called her from the hospital. She knew without asking that she'd called Chuck and Eva. "She's lucky the driver didn't sue her."

"She's lucky she's alive." Eva pursed her lips, letting her statement sink in for a moment. "She won't get sued. The weather was terrible. She told everyone it was an accident."

Ruby stared down at the wet clothes in the basket—her daughter's life, broken in pieces.

"What day did she and Tyson break up?" Ruby asked.

"Thursday morning. She called him when she got home from the hospital. He brought her flowers, and she called off the wedding."

"So she didn't jump in front of the truck because of the break-up."

"No. He was a nice guy. Really good to her."

Ruby had wanted to know if Eva had met him. It was both disappointing and a relief to know that she had.

"Listen," Eva said, pulling her purse tighter. "Something's going on with her, and I think it's been brewing for a long time. Years, even."

"Did you tell the doctors it wasn't an accident?"

"No, I'm telling you."

After Eva left, Ruby started the dryers and went up to the main level of the building. With its musty odor and chipped tile, the small front lobby felt like a bathroom. She stood at the door, where the landing on the other side jutted out like a cliff. Sirens wailed in the distance.

Ruby had grieved and suffered and found a way to move on. She'd done all of it without Chuck. And she'd done all of it without Beth. In fact, she'd found it impossible to grieve in front of her daughter. Because Beth grieved with such intensity that it almost felt fake. The very force lessened Ruby's emotions. It reminded her of her early marriage, when she'd get frustrated with the can opener or something, slamming it down, and then Chuck would come in from the garage, fuming over a lost nail or screw, and she'd go from angry to patronizing, telling him to knock it off. She'd done the same with Beth, moving from sad to impatient—drying the girl's tears and turning on some stupid TV show, or forcing her out of bed at 10 o'clock on Saturday mornings to go clothes shopping. Anything to get her out of her misery and act like a normal, happy girl.

And Beth had acted normal and happy by the time she reached high school. She'd found a group of friends, joined the girls' soccer team, volunteered at the animal shelter, excelled in math, planned a career in finance. But once she was on her own, her life had somehow crumpled and drifted like paper in the wind. Maybe something had happened in college. Or maybe not enough had happened. Either way, Beth seemed to believe she was supposed to find a way to forget about it all. And she seemed to believe Ruby already had.

She'd been gone almost an hour. Ruby hurried up to the third floor, back to Beth's apartment, suddenly conscious of how long she'd been gone. And how much can go wrong in a few minutes. She'd gone through it a million times—what if she'd gotten up just a little earlier? Checked to see if Noah was awake before she ever went downstairs that morning? Gone back up sooner?

She knocked as she opened the door to Beth's apartment, and her heart jumped—the recliner was empty, except for a pillow in the seat. The bathroom door was open; the light was off. The kitchen was dark. The windows were shut.

Ruby called for her daughter, speaking her name like a question. She tried to sound calm. It was the tone strangers used when making small talk at the bar in O'Hare or in line for the Hilton shuttle bus. *Got kids? How many?*

For a moment, silence. In the bright morning light, Beth's apartment looked like the scene of an investigation, as if someone had removed all the furniture so the police could comb the carpet for clues.

And then came the answer in that tired, refined-sugar voice. "I'm getting a clean sweatshirt." Beth appeared like a balloon in the doorway of her bedroom, tethered to one crutch. The sweatshirt was plain white. The sweatpants were the same pair she'd worn yesterday, bulging over the cast. One of Beth's hands darted into a pocket like a frightened animal and then reemerged with a tissue.

"Did you want help taking a shower?" Ruby asked, hoping the answer would be no. She hadn't seen Beth naked or even in underwear since the girl was—well, just a girl. Ruby came closer, but stayed about a body's length from her daughter.

Beth was shaking her head, it seemed, and lurching toward the recliner when she dropped the crutch. The padded under-arm support hit the wall and made a slow downward arc with a sound like an airplane passing overhead. Beth started to reach for it but gasped in pain, and that's when she started to go down. Ruby lunged, sliding one hand under Beth's massive upper arm and another around her bulging waist. The flesh was firmer than it looked. Not muscle, certainly, but not marshmallow-soft. Ruby imagined the skin underneath was soft and dry, almost powdery. Wholesome and tender. For a moment Ruby was tangling with toddlers after their bath, laughing as her cheek slid across a leg, a palm, a happy pulsing chest; nuzzling against a small, eager fore-head fringed in damp hair. But there was no scent of lavender or soap—just a faint reminder of yesterday's beans. And something garlicky, like stale hummus. Ruby floundered and caught hold, bracing herself against the wall to bear the full weight of the body. And she had it. But then she realized her hand had slid beyond Beth's armpit, and what she was holding was actually the girl's enormous bulge of a breast.

Ruby could have shifted the weight. She could have nudged a knee under Beth's thigh and adjusted the position of her hands. Or she could have just left them where they were. But instead, she pulled back, stepped back, and let go.

Beth dropped to the floor with a shrill shout. Really, the fall had only been from a height of about two feet. But she rolled onto her side and lay there like she'd been struck by a car all over again.

Ruby squatted and put a hand on Beth's arm. "Did you hit your leg?" Ruby asked, knowing she hadn't.

Beth didn't answer—just pawed at the tears streaming down her face.

"Beth."

"I landed on my bruised tailbone."

Eva hadn't mentioned that injury. Ruby stared at her hand on her daughter's arm. Beth wiped her face and looked up at her mother. The expression there wasn't shock or anger, but complete resignation. A lifelong expectation that in any given situation, her mother would always let go. This was the moment Ruby would agonize over for years to come. This is what she had to make right.

Beth turned toward the wall and they sat on the floor in the hallway for a long time. Someone in the apartment next door was grinding coffee beans. There was laughter and footsteps farther down the corridor. Sounds of traffic and a dog barking and sirens in the distance.

Eventually, Ruby spoke. "I think about him every day. Every time a thread comes loose on my clothes, I remember the way he'd stick strings in his nose when he was little, like he was fishing up there. And every time I put jelly on a piece of toast, I think of how much he loved peanut butter 'belly' sandwiches."

Beth didn't move.

"And I think about the way he died."

Beth had asked her once how he did it, and Ruby had said, simply, even impatiently, as if she should know, "With a necktie." Surely they'd told her that much before. What Ruby hadn't told her is that she still had a piece of the tie. Green silk with a pattern of tiny blue tugboats. She'd bought it for him to wear to church. She kept it in her jewelry box, and every now and then she took it out and held it.

"The technical term is autoerotic asphyxiation," Ruby said. "Cutting off the flow of oxygen while masturbating. It supposedly intensifies the feeling."

Beth turned and looked at her. "But he hung himself."

"He did," Ruby said, nodding. "By accident."

"What are you saying?"

Ruby wondered how much she really didn't know about the things people do. "If he hadn't passed out, he could have just stood up and untied himself. He'd probably done it a million times before. This was the one time it went wrong."

"I don't understand."

Ruby sighed. "He didn't commit—he didn't die by *suicide*."

"But Noah was depressed. Everyone said so." She was crying again.

"No, he wasn't."

"He listened to death metal and wore black and hardly ever came out of his room."

"So did all of his friends."

"Everyone kept saying they should have said something sooner." Beth wiped her nose on her sleeve. "His teachers, people at church, the neighbors—they all came up to me for years and said, looking back, they could see the signs. Pastor Gladstone even blamed himself. You told me that."

"People always blame themselves for the wrong things," Ruby said carefully.

"And Dad helped with those suicide awareness fundraisers."

"People asked him to participate, so he did." Ruby gently squeezed Beth's arm. "You don't believe me."

"I don't know."

"I was the one who found the body," she said. "It was obvious what he was doing when he died."

She could have described the scene. The strength she'd mustered in order to lift his body, to relieve the pressure on his thin neck, as if she could still save him. She could have explained that Chuck cut the tie like some terrible umbilical cord. That as she held the body, Chuck pulled up Noah's pants and cleaned up the scene so the police only saw part of the truth when they arrived. And that later, when she asked Chuck about the nudie magazines and other things he'd taken out of the room, he said *what things?* She must have imagined them. And so she searched the trash and the recycling and the fireplace and every drawer in the house for days, until the garbage collectors had come and gone and there's no way the things would have still been around, even if they'd existed in the first place.

"Why did you lie?" Beth asked.

"That's the thing—we didn't. Not really. Not until recent years, to people like Eva who don't already know. Because back then, the police called it a suicide, and word got out and then everyone knew without us saying a word."

"That's still lying."

"We were embarrassed. But mostly, we thought the lie wouldn't hurt anyone. And we were wrong."

Beth looked down at her leg, as if suddenly realizing her mother had been the one to push her off the sidewalk in front of a truck.

Ruby would call Chuck later that day, let him know she'd told Beth the truth. Tell him she'd stay the whole week, too. Maybe one of them would get a hotel. Or maybe one of them would sleep on the floor next to Beth's chair. And she'd finally tell him about the school counselor who'd called a few months after Noah died—the one who'd said Beth was eleven times more likely to try to kill herself because Noah had. The one whose advice Ruby had ignored, because, obviously, the woman didn't know the whole story. But none of them had.

Ruby touched her fingertips to the dirty, blueish toes sticking out of Beth's cast. They were cold. Beth didn't move. Beth had Ruby's toes—those same wide nailbeds, those familiar long half-suns sitting low on their horizons. Like the symbols on the daylight chart she kept by her kitchen window, showing the exact time of sunrise and sunset for each day in the month.

Somehow, it was already the middle of January. She hadn't thought about it, but the days must be getting longer now. She could almost feel it in her bones. Every day, a little more light.

An Hour You Don't Expect

Julie hoped her children would remember that she took them to church when they were young. She'd catch herself thinking this in the park or at the breakfast table, and she'd worry about herself. It came too easily, this thought that soon she wouldn't be there for them, that they'd have to rely on memories to know that deep down, in spite of everything else, she was good.

She began to wonder how the end would come, and cancer made so much sense that by the time she heard the diagnosis, she was only surprised it wasn't hers. Pastor Gladstone announced it one Sunday in September, staring at the floor until he'd said it all—his advanced stage, his immediate retirement—so the steadiness of his voice matched the blankness of the bald spot facing the congregation.

A few women gasped and looked at each other, confirming the gravity of the situation, but Julie kept her eyes on Pastor Gladstone. When he finally lifted his face, she got lightheaded and dropped onto the pew, right on top of Aubrey's legs, for the girl had stretched out lengthwise along the cushion. Aubrey let out a scream that made Julie think either she understood the horror of the news or one of her ankles had just snapped. Julie pulled Aubrey onto her lap, saw that she was fine, and held her tight.

"You're hurting me," Aubrey said.

Julie let go, but Aubrey was still pulling and slammed her elbow against the pew. She wailed and David watched, motionless on the other side of his sister, Pete's broken wristwatch gaping on his arm, the hands stuck at the prim angle of three o'clock.

Julie scooped up Aubrey, carried her out to the narthex, and when everything sacred and polite was behind her, she pushed the girl's ear to the carpet.

This is how Pastor Gladstone had first seen Julie—holding Aubrey flat on the ground outside the Crestfall Public Library. He'd appeared in a White Sox T-shirt and jeans and asked if Julie wanted a break. She had said those very words herself so many times—to Pete, to her mother, to the wall—that she sat back on her heels, stunned, and nodded. Let's go for ice cream, he'd said, taking each child's hand. You can come with us, if you want, he told Julie—or not, and I'll bring them back in an hour. Julie hesitated, wondering what kind of mother would leave her kids with a stranger, and what kind of man would want to take them. She followed, mostly out of curiosity. She became her own third child and he became the grandfather they'd never had, asking each of them about their favorite foods and colors. It wasn't until he walked them back to their car that he gave Julie his card with the little cross on it. There, just months after her mother's death, years into the demise of her marriage, weeks before filing for divorce, she felt a warmth like affirmation.

When Aubrey stopped thrashing and lay still on the narthex carpet, Julie released her grip and helped the girl sit up.

"You can't behave that way in church," Julie said. She smoothed Aubrey's parchment-colored hair and led her back into the sanctuary, back to David, who was openly staring at all the people wiping their eyes.

A crowd had begun to encircle Pastor Gladstone and his wife, Eileen, who had joined him at the front of the sanctuary. Eileen's quiet piety usually made Julie nervous, but today the woman's underturned bob communicated defeat instead of deference. Julie moved toward her, but so did everyone else, leaving Julie trapped at the end of the aisle, a hand on each of her children, a tourist pressing against a barricade. She backed her way out and led

Aubrey and David to the car, wondering what she could do to help the Gladstones.

Julie had never gone to church as a child, but her nearest playmates—the girls in the apartment upstairs—had. On Sunday mornings she watched them traipse down the sidewalk in their denim skirts and skip back home hours later with scribbly Sunday school crafts. For years she thought church was a remedial art class. That explained why she never went; she was good at drawing. Even her mother said so. But Julie became jealous of the girls' hand-print posters and paper-plate tambourines, and she began to wish for church the way she wished for braces and glasses and crutches and other things she never needed—thank God, her mother said.

The Sunday after she met Pastor Gladstone in the parking lot, she got up early to get the kids dressed and told Pete where they were going. He squinted from the bed and asked why. She said she needed it, they all did, but he refused to go with them. They had agreed, after all, to be a secular family. This in spite of, or perhaps because of, Pete's Catholic upbringing. So Julie took the kids alone. And what started as a Sunday morning activity quickly expanded to include several volunteer commitments a week. When Pete asked her about it again a month or so later—why the sudden full-force devotion, why everything had to be all or nothing with her—she said it's about compassion, just a little fucking *compassion*. She yelled until it didn't sound like a real word anymore.

Her prayers went that way, too—from logic to nonsense. She prayed for Pastor Gladstone's healing, but she prayed harder for the chance to be a part of his care as he died. She envisioned herself heating mugs of tea, running to the pharmacy, driving him to doctor appointments when Eileen couldn't. Or even when she could. Julie prayed to sit at his feet until the end.

But now, with the news of the illness as fresh as the bruise on Aubrey's arm, she didn't know what to do—so she did what she always had. She dropped David off at school on Monday morning, finished the layout of a client's fishing tackle brochure, and drove to church with Aubrey to clean the sanctuary. It would be good to feel useful, to feel the wrinkles that devout hands had left on photocopied psalms at the services the day before. And good to be in a place devoid of screaming. It had been a rough morning, punctuated with tears and the banging of heels on the kitchen floor, all because Aubrey wanted to eat her cereal out of the blue bowl instead of the yellow one, so Julie had shoved both goddamn bowls in the trash.

But when she got to church, the parking lot was empty and the big red door was locked. Julie stood there for a moment and then hoisted Aubrey onto her hip, as if improving the visibility of the child would convince the pastor to present himself. She knocked and waited a few seconds, just to be sure, before loading Aubrey back into the car and heading home.

Of course she'd known he wouldn't be there. He'd said he was retiring immediately. And yet a part of her had hoped Pastor Gladstone would retire from everything but her children. That Julie would still find him hunched in the tiny office that smelled like cinnamon tea and warm erasers. That she'd get Aubrey settled beside him, step back, and watch her from the doorway as if from heaven.

It was senseless to think the children would live with Pastor Gladstone if some tragedy took them from Julie, but she could envision that arrangement more easily than the kids living with Pete. He only had a studio apartment, after all. She'd never seen the inside, but he'd said it was too small to keep the kids overnight—he only took them on Saturday afternoons and Wednesday evenings, for dinner at Panera or Five Guys. Julie imagined a living space barely big enough for the bed he probably shared with an array of women met in bars. She wondered if he still got drunker than his dates, if he still liked to be taken care of.

And she wondered if she and Pete would still be together if she'd forced him out of that role, if she'd known how.

She remembered sitting on the stoop one night as a child, and the Sunday school girls coming down to ask what she was doing. Waiting, she said, and even then, even at that age, she knew she'd said too much. At least she knew not to tell them about the bearded man slumped on the sofa in her apartment. Her mother's friend. He had a headache, and he'd said Julie's voice felt like spikes driving into his skull, so she had to go sit outside. It was the first time her mother had let anyone else tell her what to do.

The window upstairs opened and a woman with an unleavened voice called the Sunday school girls inside for their baths. The girls looked at Julie. It was too late to sit alone on the stoop. If the girls told their mother, she would tell Julie's mother, and Julie would get in trouble for embarrassing her. I have to go in, too, Julie said. And she went down the hall and sat on the indoor-outdoor carpet by her apartment.

The door was open. That was Julie's fault; she hadn't shut it tight. Years later, whenever someone at church talked about the crucifixion, she thought of this moment, of the bearded man calling her bad names and passing out, appearing in every sense to be dying from her sins. Her mother there to take care of the body. The scene played out like an illustrated myth. A glass of water held to a mouth. A hand inside a waistband. An arching spine. Resurrection. If only amends were so easy.

Back at home, Julie mixed batter for a 7UP cake, a church cookbook classic. The combination of comfort and novelty seemed somehow appropriate, and she considered making the Gladstones a Coke-can chicken or Dr Pepper-glazed ham to go with it. She and Pete used to playfully argue about whether cooking with pop was a Midwestern thing or a Southern thing or just an old-person thing, and the discussion itself felt Midwestern and Southern and old.

She was thinking about this when she discovered that Pete had taken the cake pans when he moved out. She hadn't just misplaced them—the pie plate and tart pan were also gone. But he'd left the cupcake tins, stacked in the cabinet above the fridge like oversized Lego blocks. Evidently, he thought he'd have occasion to bake an array of sophisticated desserts in his limbo-white kitchenette, and she'd have nothing on the calendar but children's birthday parties. A blade of stainless-steel rage sliced through her. She poured the batter and shoved the tins into the oven, and then she dropped the dirty bowls, whisk, and spoon into a box she addressed to Pete, since he might as well have those things, too.

A couple hours later, after the post office but before David's school let out, she and Aubrey arrived at the pastor's house—an olive-green split-level with yellow mums lining the walk. She'd only been here once before, for a potluck dinner last summer, when the windows were full of light and chatter. But today, everything looked dark and sealed-off. She reached for the doorbell, thought better of it, and knocked instead, hoping—praying, even—that Pastor Gladstone would answer instead of his wife.

A long minute passed and then Eileen appeared, her hair greasy and tucked behind her ears. She wore flannel pajama pants and a pale denim work shirt sagging at her shoulders.

"I just wanted to say, I'm so sorry to hear the news," Julie said.

"Thank you." Eileen nodded once, pinching her eyes shut.

"Is—the pastor around?" It must have been weird to have a husband that others referred to by his occupation. Like a king or a plumber.

"He's taking a nap," she said. "And I'm sorry, but there will be no more services."

"Oh, I know, I was there yesterday, but I was hoping I could still see him sometimes." She worried that it sounded too intimate.

Eileen shook her head. "No more services. Please."

Confused, Julie started to protest, but stopped when she realized Eileen was staring at the cupcakes.

"7UP," Julie said, offering the plate and suddenly feeling like the only person drinking pop in a bar.

It was a paper plate, loosely covered with plastic, and it buckled as Eileen took it from her. The woman's face twisted as she lurched to regain balance, and one of the cupcakes fell, glaze-side down, on the welcome mat. Julie bent and snatched it up. She wished she'd thought of something clever to say—like, "Now it's only Six-Up!" Or even just "Five-second rule!"—but instead, she awkwardly swiped the glaze off the mat with her finger, wondering why she'd ever thought cupcakes were an appropriate offering.

"Just leave it," Eileen said, but Julie had begun plucking at the crumbs. "*Please.*"

Julie stood up and discovered something more than impatience in Eileen's eyes. In all the hours Julie had spent at the church, all the times she'd commented that the church family had become her *family*-family—Julie had never considered what Eileen must have assumed.

"You know," Julie said, lowering her voice and speaking into the mangled cupcake like a microphone. "There was never anything *romantic* going on between us."

Between me and Charles, she thought, the pastor's first name ready on her tongue, even though she'd only ever said it aloud to Pete. When Pete picked up the kids on Saturday mornings, she'd say Charles might stop by or she was meeting him for lunch, letting Pete think Charles was someone she'd met online. He might as well have been. The Charles of her fantasy was young and cultured, and she invented an entire year's worth of dates with him— things like museum outings, concerts, and wine tastings. Things she imagined Pastor Gladstone did with his wife twenty years ago.

Eileen's face flushed. "I know that," she said. Like *duh*. And something like laughter and pity pulled at the edges of her face.

"Thanks for the cupcakes," she added, tilting her head, lilting her voice, and the door closed, leaving Julie confused and embarrassed and mournful, as if Pastor Gladstone had died with the cathunk of the deadbolt.

Julie wondered if Aubrey would remember this someday— the stupid cupcakes, the pastor's wife talking to Julie like a child. But maybe Aubrey wouldn't remember the Gladstones at all. Or even that Julie and Pete had once lived together. It might be better that way.

Julie had wanted her mother to die believing Julie's marriage was perfect, but the truth had found its way into the last days.

"Pete doesn't need me for anything anymore," Julie said, rubbing her mother's wasted feet while a pot of soup warmed on the stove. "I'm not sure we were ever meant to be together."

"Oh we're *all* meant to be together," the old woman said. It was the last lucid thing she ever said.

Julie poured her mother's diluted apple juice, thinking of the Jesus man and all the ones who'd come after him—the fireman, Santa Claus, the Holy Ghost, the bank teller. She'd forgotten so much about her mother, and yet she remembered that the Jesus man's birthday was March 1st and he didn't eat beef and he smelled like bread and no matter how many times he died, her mother was always there to bring him back to life.

One morning after he left for work, Julie's mother danced around the kitchen with one of his plaid shirts, the sleeves outstretched in her arms. "He told me I'm good," she said, and his words became truth. "Your mama is *gooood*."

The next Sunday morning, David was already dressed in a sweater and his good jeans by the time Julie got up to make coffee. She explained that they wouldn't be going to church that day—that they might not ever go back—and he nodded, accepting the information with a solemnity that reminded her of Pete. Aubrey never even noticed the break in routine, and that reminded her of herself.

But they did go back to church—just not that one.

It was three weeks later, a Saturday in early December, when the kids were with Pete and Julie was running errands, when she drove past a low-slung cinderblock building she'd never even realized was a church. A mottled bride shivered on the steps above a photographer. The groom stood in the grass, scratching his neck. She almost didn't notice the man next to him, dressed in all black except for the white tooth of his clerical collar. He was younger than Pastor Gladstone, maybe in his early forties, holding a Styrofoam cup in both hands. He had a full head of dark, wiry hair and skin that held onto the sun. He turned toward the road as he sipped and seemed to look right at her, almost nodding, as if to say yes, this is the next place for you. She straightened and smiled—at him, at the bride, at the cross above the door.

The next morning she and the children climbed the steps where the bride had stood, and sat in the back on an aisle. The altar was bare wood, and the pews were padded with faded pink cushions that reminded her of a nursing home, or a Chinese buffet. The air smelled like rice. During the peace, she shook hands with the people around her. Let them believe what they wanted to about the children's absent father and the pale, pinched skin where she used to wear her wedding ring. After the service she waited in a long line to introduce herself to the pastor. When it was her turn, he took her hand in both of his, making a sandwich of it.

"Welcome," he said. "It's good to see a new face here." The bulletin said his first name was Peter. She liked the sound of it, imagined telling Pete that she'd be spending time with *Peter*.

She smiled broadly. She wondered if he recognized her from the day before, but decided he probably didn't. "I make my own hours for work, so I can do things to help on weekdays," she told him, cringing at her word choice. "Like clean, or fold bulletins."

"Oh! Well, thanks, but there's no need," he said, letting her hand go. She noticed he didn't wear a wedding ring. "We've got a cleaning crew and a new-fangled copy machine that does all that folding and stapling."

He smiled at David and Aubrey. She expected him to ask their names or offer them peppermints from his pocket, but his eyes whisked away to the elderly woman approaching behind them. She was saying something about card tables for a seniors luncheon, and he raised his eyebrows, listening, but turned back to Julie just long enough to thank her for coming, as if he were the host of an awkward dinner party. She nodded, feeling disappointed and resigned to the notion that all of us are just doing the best we can.

When she got home, she noticed a box on the porch, and it took her a moment to realize it was the same one she'd used to mail the batter-slimed baking things. Pete's address was still on the lid. He'd delivered the box in person. He must have assumed she'd be at church, at Pastor Gladstone's church. The fact that he didn't know they'd left that church made her sad.

She opened the box later that night, after the kids were in bed. And there they all were. The mixing bowls, the whisk, the wooden spoon—all clean—as well as the cake pans, the pie plate, the tart pan, nestled together like a family.

She still got emails from the old church—newsletters announcing parishioners' birthdays and donation requests and updates on Pastor Gladstone's health. He had decided not to undergo chemo. He had begun to feel tired, but didn't have any real pain yet. He and Eileen were heading to Florida with his brother for a week. When they got back, they would begin accepting home-cooked dinners. Parishioners were invited to sign up for a day on the calendar in the fellowship hall. Julie hit delete and continued bringing the kids to the cinderblock church.

It felt strange, entering the building only on Sundays, sitting with people who barely knew her first name, getting the same polite pastoral handshake as everyone else. But then it felt good. A pause in the rush of the week, a blur of anonymity. The kids did search-a-words during the service—Aubrey circling individual letters and coloring over David's found words—and Julie could pretend for a while that they belonged to the woman at the other end of the pew or the couple across the aisle who already had three kids of their own. Whenever Aubrey acted up, Julie had only to slide her hand up the girl's pant leg and press a fingernail into the soft flesh, and she went silent.

After the service each week, all the children filed into a classroom with pairs of dumb-looking animals painted on the walls. Some mothers went to adult Bible study or the grocery store during Sunday school hour, but Julie went to the forest preserve down the street. She sat with the heat blasting, facing a wall of bare maples, and watched the people who didn't spend their Sunday mornings at church. She pitied them, and she envied them.

Pastor Gladstone died on a Wednesday afternoon. The news came in a broadcast email with his name as the subject line, and she knew what the words would say before she read them. Two days later, she received the funeral information. But Julie felt no need to go. She'd already mourned the loss of this man who'd saved her from herself.

It had been different with her mother. She'd never saved Julie fom anything, but Julie had never stopped trying to save her mother from everything. Especially in the final days of cold washcloths, hot-water bottles, and mashed banana on tremulous spoons.

Julie decided she'd tell her kids about Pastor Gladstone if they asked. But they didn't. She deleted the emails, thinking of a passage the pastor had read once—something about being prepared for an hour you don't expect.

"Don't ever forget that this could all go away in a flash," he'd said with a sweep of his arm, meaning all the families and everything they held dear. It was both a threat and a promise.

The Sunday after Pastor Gladstone died, Julie was the first person to enter the sanctuary at the cinderblock church. She guided the children to the first pew and settled them in front of the pulpit, like they'd come for a loved one's funeral. Maybe Pastor Gladstone's or her mother's. Maybe her own. She felt removed from herself, as if watching not from heaven or the hallway, but from another life. When the organist began to play, Julie had to strain to hear the melancholy groans. When the acolyte bowed at the altar and tipped her flame toward the candles, Julie had to squint to see the light. The banging of Aubrey's plastic unicorn against the pew slowed until it synched with the ticking of David's watch—that stupid, ugly watch! Pete must have finally replaced the battery for him. The rhythm of her children would have bothered her any other day, but today it reminded her of peaceful things. Diligent turn signals. Retreating footsteps. Slowing heartbeats. And then the sound slipped away altogether.

At home, later that day, the doorbell rang. Julie lifted her teabag and let it drain over her mug for a few seconds before tossing it in the trash. She took one more bite of her toast, put the slice down, and then picked it back up and finished. She was still chewing when she opened the door. There was the cinderblock pastor, standing on the porch with her children. David looked solemn, staring at the welcome mat even after Julie said hello. Aubrey was jumping in place—dramatically, with a long, deep-squat windup before each vertical burst—just to hear the satisfying clap of her patent-leather shoes on the cement. The pastor kept a hand on each child, the one on Aubrey bouncing with each jump and resettling like a fly. The one on David was firm, the man's arm fully extended, holding the boy out like an example. An anecdote in a sermon. Take this child, for instance. Take this child. She'd said as much that very morning, with Aubrey on her hip. Will you take her a minute? And handed her off to a Sunday school teacher. As if by using the word "take" she could forget that she'd given her up, that she'd left David eating coffee cake in the fellowship hall and slipped out the back door.

Take this child. If not the girl, then the boy. The boy who had seemingly endless patience not only for his sister but also his mother. The boy who would look at the welcome mat for as long as it took for her to do the right thing.

"We didn't know when you'd be back," the pastor said. He was trying to sound casual—saying "when," not "if"—but Julie sensed the underlying panic. What would he have done if she hadn't been home? What if she closed the door in his face? What if she was incapacitated and he couldn't leave the children with her? She considered the questions, too, as if she were still removed from herself. And in a way, she was. She was someone she could never be—and yet had undeniably become.

"I offer pastoral services," he said. "If you'd ever like to talk—?"

In that moment she saw herself on the other side of a door, the Gladstones' door, holding a plate of cupcakes. When Eileen had said there would be no more services, she hadn't meant church services—she'd meant pastoral services. Counseling. All those hushed conversations when the kids were out of earshot. (How do you feel when the kids are with Pete?) Pastor Gladstone wasn't being friendly, he was trying to help her. (How do you feel when Pete brings the kids home?) Of course Eileen hadn't suspected an affair. Charles never could have had romantic thoughts about her because that would imply that she was desirable. She was, in fact, the opposite. She was someone to worry about.

Aubrey stopped jumping. David kept his head down and coughed, just once, into the crook of his arm like she'd taught him.

Julie wanted to push everything away and pull everything close, thinking this is what people mean when they talk about grace, and how different life would have been if her mother had experienced it.

Julie dropped to her knees and took the kids in her arms. "There you are!" she said, as if she'd only just opened the door. "I've been so worried!"

David looked up, and the muscles in his face relaxed. She hoped he would forget this day, but it would stay with him forever—along with the pleading paleness of her eyes and the thump of his heart whenever she grabbed his arm and he waited for what she'd do next.

The Ice River History Museum,
Formerly Saint Catherine's Convent

Dot hobbled along with her walker, making apologies for moving slow since her fall. The docent asked what happened, and she explained about the dark cat in the dark hallway. Then she pointed at his ankle and asked *him* what happened. He adjusted his pants leg so it covered the monitoring device. A dark man in a dark alley, he said.

The docent paused at the first room and held out his hand. This is what a nun's room looked like. Here's where she kept her vows. Here's her bed, her bible, the sink where she splashed water on her face.

Dot and her daughter Mary stood in the doorway, feeling the thickness of the barrier rope against their shins.

And here's what their chapel looked like. Here's a pew, a kneeler, an altar.

This here is the religious artifacts room. The docent gestured to a headless mannequin modeling a faded habit. A forest of crucifixes grew around her.

And the last room is the biggest one. The collected curios of Ice River's residents. There was no rope here, so Dot and Mary stepped inside and followed the docent toward the doll collection.

These are some of the finest porcelain dolls in the world, the docent said.

I used to have one just like that, Dot said, pointing to the one with chipped lips.

They wandered among bookshelves stacked high with old photo albums, paperweight fetishes, and a small herd of taxidermy—pheasants, mostly. There was Celia Smith's candlestick collection, still dripped full of wax, and Thelma Logan's wigs on plastic heads. She was the mayor's mistress in the fifties, the docent said.

Yes, I knew her, Dot said. She lumbered ahead with her walker, past the record collections and on to the display of Patty Singleton's crystal Christmas ornaments. I knew her, too, Dot said. She was a real bitch.

Mary didn't think her mother was capable of saying that word—especially in a holy place, or a place that used to be holy.

Dot moved on, pushing past the docent. Here they are, she said, stopping mid-stride so that Mary nearly ran up on her heels. My elephants. A typed card taped to the shelf explained that there were a hundred and seventy-eight of them, made of ivory and wood and stone and brass and jewels.

"These are *yours?*" Mary asked.

"Well, my goodness," the docent said. "Thank you for your generosity."

"You never asked if I wanted any of these," Mary said.

"Because you don't," Dot said. "They only have meaning for me. When I worked at the embassy, I had friends from India and Africa and all over Asia, and they sent them for me to remember them by. But they're all dead now."

"I don't think our donors have ever come in here. They're usually dead, too," The docent said. "We should interview you for the newsletter about the work you did."

"Interview my daughter," Dot said. "See if she can even tell you."

"I wouldn't know what to say," Mary said. "I'm still trying to figure out why you gave all these to a stranger instead of your only daughter." She was staring at the leg where the docent wore his monitor.

Dot pulled a small white elephant from the back of a shelf. "Here. This one is for you."

Mary turned the misshapen lump in her hand. "Great. Thanks."

"See, you don't know the value of anything. That piece is pure ivory. It's three thousand years old." Dot turned to the docent. "Bet you didn't know that, did you?"

He turned red, as though he'd been caught stealing.

Mary looked the elephant in its dull eye and tried to imagine what it had seen in its long life that started before there was a difference between things that are holy and things that are not. But she couldn't see that far, couldn't see beyond this day, this walker plodding ahead of her, this handbag into which she dropped the elephant among the things that matter.

Ozone

(O_1)

Joe

It was the seventh day of hundred-degree heat, and it was starting to feel like some kind of un-creation story. We ate bowls of chilled applesauce and went to bed at noon. Val sprayed our sheets with water and taped freeze packs to the air conditioner in the window. My electric oxygen machine hummed in the corner of our room. We did not sleep.

The brownouts started again around three o'clock. The hot woman on Val's soap opera became a flickering flame. I hit the power button and snuffed her out. It was a rerun anyway, Val said, and the same instructions kept running across the bottom of the screen. Turn off all unnecessary appliances. Stay inside. Check on your elderly neighbors. But everyone on this block was elderly, so no one checked on anyone.

The air conditioner quieted to a growl. I felt a pull in my chest and adjusted the tube in my nose. I propped myself up on pillows, but the heat kept rising like stuffing in my lungs. Whenever it got like this, I had to get out. Even if that meant out into the sun. Even though Val would only go as far as the door.

She uncoiled the tube that connected me to the machine and kept a hand on my back as I stepped onto the porch. I eased into the wrought iron chair under the awning and let the breaths come in raspy bursts like TV static. *Don't worry, the reception will get better*, I used to say when I started to wheeze, when I still had breath to spare. *Just wait for the signals to settle.* But there was no breath to spare anymore. Val stayed at the edge of the kitchen and pulled the screen door shut between us, leaving just enough room for the tube to pass. When the wheezing and coughing subsided, I patted the empty chair beside me, but she pretended not to see.

"I wonder if he'll study this," she said, meaning our son, Lou. He was an environmental scientist in California, and he was always talking about global warming. He'd called earlier this week when he heard about the heat wave setting records in Chicagoland, and we'd assured him we were fine. And we were. I was good at survival. I'd been through Korea, a few cases of Evan Williams, near-divorce, the death of our daughter, the removal of half my left lung, a car fire, and two tornadoes. I knew the emphysema was what would finally do me in. It was kind of nice to know.

"You just want him to come," I said. Come fix the air conditioning, buy us a generator, and let her bake him a chicken pot pie. "We should go there. Cool off by the ocean."

She ignored me. Lou called it air-goraphobia, what she had. She wouldn't go to the mailbox, much less the West Coast.

I breathed in as deep as I could and felt my chest expand. I missed the magnolias that used to shade this street and the fresh eggs we bought from the chicken farm until the owners died and it was bulldozed. People had complained about the chicken shit, but it never bothered me. It smelled real. Now, with its culverts and three-hour rush hours, the neighborhood reeked of prestige and progress and other things it was not.

One of the mailboxes down the street began to move. I blinked and saw it was Tommy, the kid who lived with his grandmother on the next block. Though he wasn't a kid any more than he was a mailbox. He was a tall skewer pulling a marshmallow on a leash.

"You shouldn't be out in this heat," I said when Tommy turned up our driveway.

"Neither should you," he said. He waved to Val and lifted the pup onto my lap. Tommy shifted his weight and worked his lips against his teeth. He'd be kissing girls in another year.

"I still scare you," I said. "After all this time."

Tommy's cheeks flushed. He'd once told me I remind him of his father, and I'd told him he reminds me of my son.

Lou was only fourteen when he asked what happens when you fear the thing you need to live. The air. The sun. The person who's supposed to protect you.

We all find out eventually, I'd said, shrugging off the chills he gave me. I deserved it, though, his cold stare. I'd missed out on three years of his childhood. I couldn't remember much of what happened during that time—just a blur of whiskey and women—but I knew he could. You can't make up for something like that, no matter how hard you try.

"You seen the coyote around lately?" I asked Tommy now, rubbing the pup's ear like a rabbit's foot.

"Day afore yesterday," he said. "Running in the alley behind our house."

Guess my shot hadn't hit it.

"You keep him away from that beast," I said, handing the pup back to the boy. I could feel the sweat on my leg where it had sat. "You stay safe, too," I added, adjusting my tube. "And look out for your grandma."

"Yessir." Tommy wiped his brow and went back down the driveway with the pup blurring beside him.

I watched him go, him attached to the pup and me attached to the machine and the machine attached to the wall socket.

Just before suppertime, the brownout became a blackout. I felt the drowning sensation in my lungs, thinking at first that the tube must have gotten a kink in it. I smoothed it in my hand like a piece of shoestring licorice, but that didn't help. I hauled myself up out of the chair, went inside, and saw that the clock on the microwave was dark. I called for Val, but she didn't answer. Then I heard the slosh of her shifting in the tub—she kept it full of cool water for quick dips throughout the day—and I wondered if she was drowning, too. There was a window in the bathroom, so she wouldn't have turned on the light or noticed the power shutting off.

A few years ago we saw a news segment about how every household should come up with a secret word to use in case of emergency. We tossed some ideas around until we realized we could just use "help," but we went on with the suggestions until we were laughing so hard the syllables came in spurts. *Pancake. Barbiturate. Beaverlick, Kentucky.*

I pushed the bathroom door open and peered in. Val clutched the shower curtain to her neck in modesty, as if it would be anyone but me.

I didn't have to say anything. She knew.

She heaved out of the water like a great, smooth fish and wrapped her wet body around mine. Holding me up by the elbows and armpits, she staggered with me, dripping, toward the bed. It felt like we were finally melting.

Val pulled the tube away from my face. Reattached me to the oxygen tank I'd kept in case something like this happened. Opened the valve. Adjusted the flow meter. The oxygen hushed, reassuring us, and I breathed. No electricity required. But eventually the air got trapped in the mucous clogging my lungs. Val misted the sheet she billowed over me, and suddenly I was a boy again, helping my mother pull the laundry from the clothesline at the start of a rainstorm. I was a boy being tucked into bed. I was a boy getting pummeled on the playground, my sweatshirt held over my nose and mouth until I pushed with strength I didn't know I had and sat up in the dirt, gasping.

But this time I had to fight the adrenaline. I would be okay if I stayed still and calm. The power wouldn't be out for too long. The tank would buy me five hours. That would be enough. It had to be.

I willed the oxygen to fill me, but the stuffing in my lungs seemed to expand.

I hadn't been to bed without supper in fifty years, but I couldn't have eaten if I'd wanted to.

Val tried to stay awake and I tried to sleep. But when I closed my eyes, I saw the fear on Tommy's face, on Lou's face. The nervous twitch of the pup's whiskers. The coyote in the crosshairs. I reached for the alarm clock, thinking I'd set it in case we both nodded off, but of course its face was blank.

Val's breaths came in heavy, apple-scented puffs.

I'd watched her sleep like this the day I came back home. The day she called to tell me a car jumped the curb and our daughter was dead. The day that ended the three-year separation that sat like a blank space in our marriage. In that time Val had gotten thinner, and I'd gotten fatter. We'd both grown old and pale.

It took months for us to get used to me being there and Casey being gone.

"I still can't believe you're back," Val used to say. "You're a ghost."

I was. Lou was still afraid of me, even though I kept telling him I was back for good.

One day I asked if Val wanted to visit any of our old haunts. Maybe that old truck stop near Sycamore that served the best pecan pie you ever tasted. But no, she couldn't. She said the last time she walked out the door, she lost her daughter. She wouldn't leave again.

But I walked out the door to work every day for thirty more years. Some days I almost didn't come back. It was the same way now for the air in my lungs. I was forced to sit at the door like Val, waiting, hoping, and welcoming home each breath like the prodigal son. I deserved that fate. It's dangerous territory, thinking of what people do and don't deserve.

Val's stomach rose and fell, a dark contour under a damp sheet, and I thought again of the pie, and then swimming pools. The house smelled like chlorine, like those long-ago summer nights at downtown hotels with women who had no clue what I'd left in order to be with them.

The breathing in was getting harder.

The breathing out felt like sparklers on the Fourth of July.

At some point the air was going to leave for good, taking me with it. The word "freedom" came to mind. Not my freedom, but Lou's and Val's. If I wasn't around, maybe he'd visit more often. Maybe he'd convince her to step outside her fear. Maybe it wouldn't take much convincing. Because here was *my* fear: that I was the real reason she'd stayed inside all this time. Keeping house, keeping vigil. Knowing I'd always come home as long as I knew she depended on me for groceries.

It's a hard thing, realizing that your absence has more value than your presence—that you can protect your family more as a memory than in the flesh.

I touched Val's arm, sticky with sweat.

"I'm so sorry," I said.

She didn't stir.

After a while I pulled the phone off the nightstand and dialed Lou's number. I waited, picturing him on a couch. It bothered me that I didn't know what color to make it in my head. I waited longer, thinking of the three-hour time difference, but the phone didn't even ring. I tried again, but then I realized there was no dial tone. It was a cordless phone, useless without electricity, the batteries gone dead hours ago.

Val slept soundly, and I decided, conclusively, not to disturb her.

The reception will get better, I thought, feeling the air rattle in my chest.

Just wait for the signals to settle.

(O₂)

Tom

Every time I walked past the Martins' driveway, I had to yank on
the leash to keep Blanco from turning in and begging for an ear
rub. It went like that for weeks, until one day there was an extra
car parked out front. We walked by half a dozen times to scope
out the situation. Someone stood in the kitchen window. A man.
Then one of the times we passed, the man was standing by the
mailbox, waiting for us.

"I keep seeing you," he said. He looked just like Mr. Martin,
but with hair and without tubes, his face only beginning to crease.
Blanco jumped up and pawed his calf.

"Sorry about your dad," I said.

"You must be Tommy."

I didn't bother explaining that I wished people would call me
Tom. In two days I was going to go live with my dad, and none of
this would matter.

"I was hoping I'd get to meet you," he said. "I could use your
help, if you got a minute."

I'd never been inside the Martins' house. It reminded me of
a hospital with its pale green walls and sheets tucked around
the couch cushions. An oxygen tank sat in the corner like a kid
in time out. Mrs. Martin stood in the kitchen, cutting a green
pepper into postage stamps. I'd never seen her without a screen
between us, and I saw now that she might have been pretty at
one time.

"You'll eat lasagna and salad," she said, not asking. "Lou
brought chocolate milk." She smiled, as if she somehow knew it
was my favorite thing. I wondered if my grandma had told her,
maybe at the funeral a couple weeks ago. I imagined the two
women talking about me, and it made me wish I'd been there so
they wouldn't have been able to do that. I'd been surprised my

grandma went, since she only knew the Martins by name. And I'd been surprised Mrs. Martin went, since she never went anywhere. But I guess you can't skip your own husband's funeral. My grandma said the woman brought her blue armchair to the funeral parlor and sat in it all night. I spotted it by the window now and imagined her sitting there, watching me walk Blanco past her house every day.

"That chair will be the last to go," Lou said, following my gaze. "For now we just have to box up the books."

I didn't see any books.

"Will he eat some plain hamburger meat?" Mrs. Martin asked, pointing at Blanco.

"He'll eat anything," I said, setting him on the kitchen floor and unhooking his leash.

I left Blanco eating out of Mrs. Martin's hand and followed Lou down the hall to a library that smelled like peanuts.

"You get to guess which books belonged to which person," he said. He hefted cardboard from a stack in the corner and began shaping it into boxes with a screeching tape gun.

"Your mom," I said, pulling a row of bird guides off a low shelf. The words sounded like the punch line to a joke.

"Nope. Me." I thought he was joking then, but he didn't smile.

I settled the books in a box and moved on to the thick leather-bound classics. "Your dad."

"Nope. My mom."

When I got to the environmental volumes with titles about atmospheric gases and molecular structure, I paused. "These are yours."

He shook his head. "My dad bought those. Said he wanted to understand what I do."

"What *do* you do?"

Lou sat back on his heels and thought for a second. "I study contradictions. Like how ozone is good when it's up in the atmosphere, but bad when it's down close to you. How we take in goods and give off poison."

It made me feel weird, like he knew about every Coke can I'd thrown in the trash instead of the recycling.

I moved on to an old set of encyclopedias that looked like they'd never been read.

When we finished boxing the books, we carried them to the back door and sat down for dinner. No one asked me to wash my hands or take off my hat or say grace.

"We should have been having you over for dinner this whole time," Mrs. Martin said. I was thinking the same thing. Blanco lay curled up in the blue armchair like it belonged to him.

"When are you moving?" I asked.

"I'm moving?" she asked.

Lou closed his eyes and shook his head like he was trying to get rid of a yellow jacket. "Not till you're ready," he said, opening his eyes. "We've talked about this. I'm just going to pack a few things every time I visit so it's not overwhelming later."

She looked relieved. I wondered if they'd have to move the house with her in it.

"*I'm* moving," I said. "Day after tomorrow. To Florida, with my dad." So far, I'd only told my two friends at school and my home-room teacher. I felt like I still needed practice saying the words.

"How will that be?" Lou asked.

"Hotter than blazes," I said, using my grandma's phrase, and immediately wishing I hadn't. I imagined Mr. Martin being steamed alive in his bed. But Lou just laughed. He sounded like his dad, but without the coughing. I wondered if it would be like this in Florida, laughing over dinner.

Lou and I ate bowls of chocolate ice cream on the couch while Mrs. Martin cleared the table. "I was never close with my father," Lou said. "That's how it goes sometimes between fathers and sons. It's nothing like what you see on TV."

"I don't know much about mine," I said. I tried to picture him in my head, but all I saw was Mr. Martin, plugged in like a lamp.

"I wish it had been different," Lou said.

"So did he," Mrs. Martin said, appearing in the doorway with a jar of cherries. She dropped one into each of our bowls. Lou stared at his for a moment like it might explode.

That night I packed my own books into an old duffel bag. They were just the stained second-hand novels my grandma bought me for English class. Books that had belonged to everyone. I didn't even want them anymore, but without them all I had was thrift-shop clothes. Enough to fill the floral suitcase my grandma said I could keep, as if I'd want it.

She'd gone to work and left me a frying pan of burned stew meat, along with a note telling me to empty the dishwasher. I carried the pan out to the side yard and flung its contents into the night, like they do in lacrosse. The meat rained through the trees. Then I waited, wondering if I'd hear the coyote padding through the brush.

I'd been feeding it ever since it showed up in our neighborhood. Ever since Mr. Martin began threatening to shoot it, telling me it would eat Blanco if it got the chance. The food was a peace offering and the only secret I had. I tried not to worry about what the coyote would do without me around. At least Mr. Martin was gone, too. I felt bad that part of me was glad about that.

I wondered if my father had ever shot anything. I thought about what Lou said, about those fathers on TV. I didn't play baseball or soccer or football. I was no Cub Scout. I'd never been fishing. I hoped that wouldn't be a problem.

I'd only talked to my father twice on the phone since my grandma told me I'd be moving in with him. She told me he read ads over the radio for a living, and that's what he sounded like. Excited about me the way he'd be excited about meatball sandwiches and clearance sales. *Everything must go.* It made me feel like a prize.

Tomorrow came and went, and then it was the next day. I brushed my teeth over the pink sink for the last time, put my toothbrush in a baggie and zipped it into the suitcase. I put Blanco's food and Milk-Bones in a grocery bag. I tried to make room in the duffel bag for my other pair of sneakers, but in the end I stuffed them in the garbage. I brushed my hair and then Blanco's. We sat by the door like outgoing mail.

He was supposed to be here at noon. But the phone rang at two o'clock, and my grandma answered it. She didn't have to say anything. I knew. He just needs a little more time, she said. Give him another couple months to get ready. Then we'll figure something out.

She got me a hamburger from Petey's for dinner because she felt bad for me, but then she had to go to work. I ate half of the burger alone at the kitchen table and stopped when I remembered the commercials. *Petey's puts a smile on every face.* The tingling started in my nose and I knew what would come next, so I pinched off a piece of meat for Blanco, ran outside, and hurled the rest of the burger into the woods with so much force, it felt like my arm went with it. I sat on the grass, breathing hard and listening to the racket of the cicadas and the waves of traffic on Ogden Avenue, wondering what it would be like to live on the Gulf or the ocean—I wasn't sure which side he lived on—where the water wasn't too polluted for swimming. I wanted to live anywhere other than this frayed edge of a city where nothing happened but blow-out sales and spelling bees and ozone alerts. But I was beginning to realize I'd never get to leave.

A twig snapped, and I held my breath.

I imagined the coyote sniffing my hamburger, holding one paw up like Blanco did, and then swallowing it whole. Assuming it was there for him, as if hamburgers grew on trees. Didn't that animal know how hard my grandma worked to pay for that and everything else I ate, and all the schoolbooks and shoes and clothes I kept growing out of? Didn't he know how hard it was to take in a boy and dog no one planned on having? I picked up a rock and threw it where I'd thrown the hamburger. Then I threw another and another, sending them crashing into the darkness and ripping through the leaves and shutting up the cicadas, wanting to wrap my arms around the furry neck of this creature I'd protected, but also wanting it dead.

Later, after Blanco ran away, I'd think back on this moment and wonder if my tantrum is what made him leave—if this was the universe's way of telling me I didn't deserve him, and if the same kind of thing had happened to my father.

(O₃)

Lou

When I arrived on Thanksgiving morning I assumed there'd at least be pie, but the refrigerator was practically empty. I hadn't eaten since breakfast in Sacramento. I found a piece of grocery-store coffee cake sitting on a plate by the stove and picked it up, thinking it was for me, but it had clearly been there a while.

"I set that out for your father," Mom said. "Don't look at me that way. *He's back.*"

Those two words. She'd said them thirty years ago when he reappeared after Casey died. *Your sister is gone, but your father—he's back.* Like it was a fair trade.

"Mom."

"I always hoped he'd come back to haunt me." She dropped the coffee cake in the garbage and set the dish in the sink. "Last time I left a piece of this out, it was gone in the morning. Guess he knows it went stale."

I knew then I'd made the right decision about bringing her home with me at the end of this long weekend. I was still surprised she'd agreed. It would be hard, but she couldn't keep living like this.

"You've been through a lot of change this year," I said.

"You say that like I don't know what change is." She wiped the counter, even though it was spotless. Her arm had never been so thin.

I wanted to point out that she hadn't left the house since I was a boy. But I knew better.

"Why don't I go get us a turkey," I said.

She shook her head. "I had Tommy bring one last week."

I opened the freezer and saw the Butterball sitting in a nest of TV dinners. It would take two days to thaw.

I told her I'd get the mail, and I came back with a roasted turkey, mashed potatoes, green beans, a fifth of Jack, a bag of rolls and a pumpkin pie, all from the deli down the street. She put out the fancy plates with the gold edging and we ate, trying not to look at the empty chairs beside us.

When we'd each had seconds, she put down her fork and stared at me. "I guess my point is, I can't leave now that he's back."

"He'll know where to find you," I said. I remembered her saying the same about Santa Claus the year she took Casey and me to visit a cousin in New York for winter break. We'd left a plate of gingersnaps on the counter with a note explaining where we were.

That was the last trip we took together. Two days after we got back was when Casey died.

"What will I do in Sacramento?" she asked.

"What do you do here?"

She motioned to the boxes lining the hallway. She'd labeled them in her explicit cursive. *Holiday Kitchen Towels. Hairbrushes and Cosmetics. Candlesticks and Table Linens.*

"Plus, I'll be in the way of your personal life," she said.

I didn't tell her that my days of hosting activists at my condo were over. I hadn't been to a rally in years. And she'd stopped asking me about girlfriends long ago, so I didn't bother telling her I'd just broken up with someone. Maybe she would use the tea bags and shower gels I kept finding in my cupboards.

"It's only temporary," I said. "Till we find you your own place."

I mixed a whiskey and ginger in a coffee mug.

"We used to have cocktails by the window overlooking the backyard," she said. "We used to see deer."

I handed her the mug and she smiled, taking a sip. "You buy the good stuff," she said.

I mixed another one for myself and we took our drinks to the back window. Dad's old Winchester .22 still hung like a branch above the valance, the way it had for as long as I could remember. He'd taken it down once when I was in grade school, before he left, and made me shoot a rabbit in the woods behind the house. For years it was the worst thing I'd ever done.

"We'll have to find someone to take the gun," I said. "But who knows if it still works."

"It does. Dad used to shoot coyotes. Got one about a year ago."

I stared at her. "From the *window?*"

She nodded. "Shot at least two of them that way."

I imagined him tied to his oxygen machine, squinting down the barrel. All I could think was how lucky for him that he hadn't ended up in jail. And how lucky for the neighbors that they hadn't ended up dead.

"There's one living back there now that's the biggest we've ever seen. Dad went after it for months, but kept missing it."

I used to tell people I went into conservation to make up for my father. But whatever I did would never be enough. He'd caused too much damage.

I could still hear the sound of the door slamming when he left, the way it made Casey and me jump. The silence that followed.

"Did he ever tell you what happened during those three years he was gone?" I asked.

She didn't answer for a long while. "It's what you'd expect."

I hadn't expected anything at the time. I was eleven. What did a man do in the world if he didn't have a wife and kids? He'd put on his shoes, go to work and take his shoes off when he got back home. That's what he did. The rest was emptiness.

Three years of emptiness.

And then one day I was twelve, playing flag football after school when the call came. My teacher came out and yelled my name on the sidelines, and I thought she was cheering me on. Cheering, of all things! I'd had a crush on her.

She yelled again and motioned me to come. Told me there was some bad news, that she needed to take me to the hospital. By the time we got there, Casey was gone.

When I woke up the next morning, he was standing at the kitchen sink. Here, in this house. Where he knew he needed to be.

"He's gone, but he's not," I said. The oxygen tank sat in the corner like an apparition.

"That's it exactly." She turned to me. "Like air."

"Same as when he was alive," I said, feeling the old anger rise inside me. I was a little boy again, wanting my father but not wanting the disappointment.

He'd tried with me, organizing hunting and camping trips, but I was too old by then and the silence between us remained. And with it, the fear. Fear that he'd drink too much again, slam the door again, leave again. On my own, I knew I wouldn't be enough to keep him there. And I wasn't enough to help my mother leave, then or now.

"He was a sad man," she said.

I started to argue, but stopped. I'd never thought of his quietness as sadness.

The wind picked up and set the maples swaying. It was like a silent movie, watching them move on the other side of the glass. The lights of the neighbors' houses winked on and off as the branches passed in front of them.

"I can't leave," she whispered.

This was going to be harder than I'd thought.

"I scheduled the cleaners to come next week," I said. "The house is supposed to go on the market as soon as possible."

I saw the fear in her eyes, and something shifted.

"You don't really believe he's back," I said. "It's just your excuse."

"It's not an excuse. It's gratefulness." She set her glass on the coffee table and looked at it instead of me. "Maybe in the morning you'll feel it, too." She got up and went to bed.

If I felt grateful for anything, it was for people who offered more than just their presence. And for people who demanded more than that from others. But if I said any of this to my mother, she'd just ask why I didn't have a girlfriend. I couldn't tell her how long it had taken me to start expecting more out of people than she ever did. Or that I knew, deep down, that my father had stopped expecting more out of me. That he'd felt my absence, too, all these years since I'd left home. And that I'd enjoyed the pain it caused him.

I finished my drink and hers.

Something moved in the bushes. Something pale and scrappy, sniffing. A scavenger looking for leftover thanksgiving.

Casey and I were walking to Petey's for hamburgers one day after school when she stopped on the sidewalk and pointed to where some men were laying bricks for a new office building.

"That's *him*," she said, and I knew right away who she meant.

We ran up to the chain-link fence, curled our fingers around the metal and watched our father smooth mortar the way our mother frosted cakes. He was tanner than I remembered, and more muscular, but he had the same round face and hair the color of our lawn in August.

Casey shouted something, and then I did too, but as he turned the muscles in his jaw reconfigured and he became someone else's father. Someone taller and happier and younger than ours. He squinted and gave an uncertain wave, as if he could almost remember us from a dream. Then he went back to work and we walked on to Petey's, though we weren't hungry anymore.

She was lucky she never knew she had to die in order for him to come home.

The animal moved along the edge of the woods. I slid a finger under the lip of the window and pulled. There was no screen. I breathed in the wind, stood and reached for the gun. The safety wasn't on. I was a boy again, crouching in the brush with my father breathing whiskey in my ear. A twig snapped under a paw.

You can't make up for everything that goes wrong, but you can do some things.

I pulled the trigger. The smudge of fur recoiled and slipped between the trees like a fog.

The wind calmed later that night, and a new silence closed in. A boy walked along the street with a leash coiled in his hand, calling for the color white. Like calling for absence. A coyote padded along Ogden Avenue, fat, strong, unafraid of the cars and the people and all that they do. A widow glanced at her adult son sleeping on the couch and wished she could help him understand her fears. How easy it is to spend a lifetime protecting ourselves from the wrong things.

She nudged the front door open, tested the air with her bare toes, and stepped outside, the cement patio biting her tender feet.

She sat in the wrought iron chair and strained to feel the imprint of her husband's body through the cool metal. She lifted her face as if waiting for a signal. Approval to stay or permission to leave.

It wasn't your fault, she said, looking at the sky. It was never as simple as that.

She filled her lungs and held the autumn air as long as she could before letting go.

What If You're Wrong

She thinks it won't happen this time, but it does. As soon as her eyes close and her body opens, she remembers the girl named Lectra. Hair bright as lightning, a storm of fear breaking across an already sodden face. The memory strikes like a commandment. Sarah's muscles tighten, and she heaves the chest bearing down on hers. She's out of bed, out of the room, before Carson can ask what's wrong.

Sarah pulls on her clothes and leans, trembling, against the floor-to-ceiling window in the dark living room. She only bought the place because her uncle gave her a good deal—he owns this near-empty building overlooking the Metra station, so far from the city that you can only see the Willis Tower on clear days if you squint. The sun has been setting earlier every day, and the gridline of the tracks brings order to the night in a way that comforts her.

She'll blame it on the newness of their relationship; she'll say she's not ready. She won't tell him she hasn't slept with anyone in four years, that abstinence became a rule for her life the way no drinking always has been. He'd think her a prude, and he'd be shocked to know the truth.

He's tugging the sheets with the same impatience of the wind whipping the banner outside—Penthouse Units Still Available!—when her mother's hatchback pulls into the parking lot. Sarah remembers her phone's relentless vibrating and grabs it off the coffee table. Two missed calls. A text message: *OK if I come for the dish?* That goddamn dish.

"My mother's here," she says, turning on the lamps. The room smells like crab rangoon and sweat.

Carson swaggers out of the bedroom, rubbing his eyes like it's morning. He looks around, as if he expects to see that her mother has been sitting on the couch this whole time. Sarah tosses him his shirt.

"You'll let me meet her?" he asks. "You're not going to stuff me in the closet till she leaves?"

"No, you can meet her." She's glad they have something to talk about besides what just happened—or didn't happen—between them. But Lectra is still on her mind. Sarah wonders if she finished at UIC, if she still lives in the city. Sarah moves around the room, shuffling the junk mail into a neat pile on the ottoman and stacking their empty takeout boxes on the kitchen counter. She puts Carson's beer bottles—three already—in the recycling bin and hides them under yogurt cups.

"You seem nervous." He flops on the couch. "Don't worry; your mother will love me." He stretches his arms along the top of the cushions and displays his easygoing grin, the one that got him the job at the country club and sent a shiver down her spine when she met him in the staff room.

"How do you know?" She gives him a coy smile. She doesn't care if her mother likes him or not. She just doesn't want to have to tell Carson what the dish is for.

"I just do. Just like I know we'll eventually fuck."

She's in awe of his certainty—of anyone's certainty about anything. Politics, morals, God, guilt. The jury that convicted her brother only deliberated for forty minutes. Not that she questions their decision. She always knew what Jerry was capable of. Her mother did not. Does not. Won't believe it's true. Sarah's mother asked Jerry's attorney why he wanted more women on the jury—wouldn't they favor Lectra? And he said no, today's women think rape victims are weak. They'd take Jerry's side. But, Sarah wondered—still wonders—what about girls who like having their hair pulled, their throats squeezed, and their bodies beaten? Are they weak, too? She can still feel the exhilarating pain. She's afraid of how much she liked it, but also afraid she didn't actually like it at all.

Carson is right about Sarah's mother; she loves him. Sarah can see it in her eyes from the moment they shake hands.

"I don't mean to interrupt!" she says, looking from Carson to Sarah. The redness of her nose and cheeks reminds Sarah of old times, when the color meant more than cold weather.

"It's fine. We just finished eating," Sarah says, pointing to the takeout boxes. "I was going to call you back when we were done."

"I was starting to worry something might be wrong," her mother says. "But clearly it's not!"

"Carson is a server at the club, too," Sarah says, as if she invited him over so they could compare notes from work.

"Oh, all those fancy country club dinners," her mother says, lifting her little finger as she sips from an imaginary wine glass. "You must deal with some very interesting people."

"That's one way to put it," Carson says, smiling.

Sarah will hear about this for weeks, how charming he is, how his hair is the same shade of gold as his skin, his hands look like molded rubber—free of the ragged, overgrown cuticles her mother hates. Sarah will say yes, she's noticed. He's also a big-band crescendo, a fist in the air, a touchdown celebration. Her mother would never understand how wrong he is for her. But Sarah could bring home a garbage can and her mother would set a place for it at the table.

"It's all about the Three Steps of Service," Carson continues, quoting the GM. "Warm greeting, anticipation of needs, fond farewell. Even if you want the fourth step to be a kick in the pants." He leans forward for this last part, saying the words in a hushed tone.

Sarah's mother laughs her big, toothy laugh. Sarah wants to pull her away, explain that Carson is flirting with her, that he's a player and—yes, she'd admit it—a drunk, and she should want better for her daughter. But her mother would just laugh again and say, well, if he's so wrong for you, why are you with him? Because, Sarah realizes now, he and Jerry would have been friends. Carson could have been any of the neighborhood boys who spent every weekend playing video games in the basement with Jerry when they were teenagers.

"Let me get the dish before I forget why I'm here," Sarah's mother says. "You must know I'm just beside myself about Jerry coming home."

Sarah goes to the kitchen, wincing at the mention of the name.

"The dinner gives me something to focus on," her mother continues, talking louder. "Something to keep me busy so I don't go crazy with anticipation."

Sarah dumps the popcorn kernels out of the dish on top of the microwave, wipes it with a towel, and brings it to her mother. "Here, the rare white, medium-sized bowl. Be careful—if you break it, you'll never find another."

"I know it's nothing special," her mother says. "But it's the perfect size for that cheese dip he loves so much. And hey, it belongs to me, and I want it back." She makes a show of clutching it to her chest.

Sarah shrugs. She wants her mother gone. And she wants Carson gone.

"Who's Jerry?" he asks.

"My brother," Sarah says, hurriedly. She can't manage to say anything more.

She picks at a loose thread on her cuff, ignoring her mother's stunned expression. The woman tells everyone with a pulse about Jerry and his wrongful imprisonment, so it's unimaginable that her daughter would work with someone, much less invite him over, and never even mention she has a brother. For a moment Sarah fears her mother will explain it all, her version of it—the drinking, the snowstorm (remember how bad it was that winter?), the way one thing leads to another (they're kids!), even if Lectra didn't mean for it to. And if she starts in, so help her God, Sarah will explain something, too—all the nights she and Jerry ate crackers for dinner as kids while their mother lay passed out on the couch, her face and arms blotched boyfriend-blue, and the Christmas when Jerry sat on the roof in the snow, drinking shots with the chimney and screaming at the neighbors, and the night he was verging on drunk by the time he left for that party in the city, how he drank another couple beers on the drive there, and how Sarah wasn't a bit surprised when the cops came looking for him the next morning.

Sarah's mother grabs her arm hard, like maybe Sarah really did say those things out loud and her mother wants to shut her up—but all she sees in her eyes is desperation. "You'll come to Jerry's welcome-home dinner, right?" she asks.

So this is the real reason she's here, to make Sarah promise face-to-face. Because in four years, Sarah has never visited Jerry. Her mother has gone every week, coming home with reports of his weight loss and graying hair, saying Sarah won't recognize him, but Sarah isn't worried. She's only afraid he thinks she hasn't come because she hates him for what he did. But it's not that. It's not that at all. She keeps trying to explain it to Jerry in a letter, but it never comes out right. What she wants him to know is there's a thin line between doing wrong and being wronged, and they're both on the same side of that line—even if the only person Sarah has hurt is herself. And she doesn't know how to move past it any more than Jerry.

"I don't know if it's best—" her mother continues. She nods toward Carson, not wanting to seem impolite by excluding him. "I think he'd just want family there, but I'm not sure." Her whole face twitches with uncertainty. Sarah remembers what it was like to study that face as a child, to search her eyes for dullness, parse her words for slurs, sniff her breath for fumes—triumphing in every hint of sobriety, ultimately forfeiting to the truth.

"Jesus, you think I won't go unless he's invited?" Sarah huffs and shakes her head. "Of course I'll be there."

"Thank you. Saturday, five o'clock." She moves toward the door with the dish in the crook of her arm like an infant. Sarah can tell she's already checked this off a mental list and her thoughts have moved on to what's left to buy, clean, and cook. Four years ago, Sarah would have offered to help. Now her mother knows not to even bother asking.

"I should take off, too," Carson says, and Sarah is relieved.

"Don't let me break up the party!" Sarah's mother looks genuinely worried.

"We both have to work tomorrow," Sarah says.

The three of them say their goodbyes without touching. Carson walks out with her mother, the two of them moving like allies. This is how it'll be from now on, her mother at Jerry's side. She'll help him redecorate his childhood bedroom, buy a new wardrobe, find a job, push his wrongdoings into the past. Sarah closes her door and leans against it for a moment, listening to their polite voices echo in the hallway. She wonders if the middle-aged banker down the hall—the only other person who lives on this floor—is home and listening, too.

Sarah goes to the window and watches Carson and her mother reappear in the parking lot. They exchange affable waves and climb into their cars. They drive away in opposite directions. The only car left is hers. Even the wind has disappeared. Finally alone, Sarah can relax. She sits at the far end of the couch, tucks her legs under a blanket, and hopes there'll come a day when this isn't the only way of life that feels right.

The Family Room

Karen hadn't planned on moving in with Ken. They'd met through work and had only been dating a few months when he closed on his new house. But then she got laid off and couldn't afford her apartment or child care anymore. She'd have to move somewhere, so why not here? Besides, Willie would start kindergarten in another year and the schools were better on this side of town. It only makes sense, Ken said, extending a diplomatic palm. We'll all move in at the same time. So he hired two teams of movers one Saturday morning in March, and by Sunday night they had formed a household. It sounded functional, tidy, contained—but the place was as jumbled as the warehouse at her old job. Boxes overflowed like filing cabinets. Dirt darkened the floors like scuffs on a loading dock. Every surface was stacked high with inventory.

She was surprised when Ken went to work first thing that Monday, leaving her to unpack and organize his house. He couldn't take time off now, with all the new business in the pipeline. She used to help manage his leads during busy times when he was her client. If she couldn't do that anymore, at least she could do this. She could try, anyway. She sliced open a box, pulled out the contents, and put them back. She'd have to make some space before she could put away his financial investment guidebooks and dietary supplements. And he'd need a whole room just for his computer parts. The man had enough power cords to weave a blanket.

Three days into the unpacking, a FedEx box appeared on the porch, something from a pharmaceutical company addressed to the previous owner. Karen almost stepped on it when she went outside for a smoke. It must have arrived while she was in the shower because she never heard the doorbell. When she called FedEx, they told her to leave the box on the porch for pickup, and it sat there for days while everyone who visited tried to bring it inside for her. The Welcome Wagon lady. The insurance rep. The next-door neighbor.

"Looks like something came for you already," the neighbor said, handing over the FedEx box and a bottle of wine with a bow on top.

Karen explained about the box and set it back on the porch as she introduced herself. She made Willie shake the woman's hand—Denise, her name was—before he ran upstairs to the full-size bed Ken had ordered back when he thought the boy's room would be a guestroom. It was Willie's first adult piece of furniture, and he spent an hour at a time perched there, bouncing among the toys she'd unpacked for him. The way the box springs creaked reminded her of sex, and she hoped Denise wasn't thinking it, too.

Karen turned the bottle of wine in her hands, admiring the label as if she knew how good the grapes were in Indiana last year. "Ken's at work," she said, not bothering to explain who he was in relation to her. It struck her then how funny the words Ken and Karen sounded together, like characters on a sitcom. It was basically the same name, except hers had a puff of air in the middle. He was lean and efficient, like precooked chicken. She was lightly breaded and still wandering around the farm with her head cut off, pretending to be a wife, a homemaker and other things she wasn't.

"By the way, the man who used to live here was a real screw-up." Denise lowered her voice. "Bill Miller. He was always getting into arguments with his wife. She'd stay away for weeks at a time. They finally got divorced, which is why they sold the house."

Ken hadn't said anything about the people who used to live here. Karen glanced at the FedEx box with sudden concern about what might be inside.

"Glad to know the new owner will fit in better," Denise said, putting a hand on Karen's shoulder as she turned to leave.

It took a second for Karen to realize Denise was talking about her. Denise waved and crossed the lawn on tiptoe. The package remained on the top step, the cardboard thick on one side from yesterday's rain. It looked suspicious, like what they warn you about in logistics training. Karen called FedEx again.

"I really need you to pick up that package today," she said. "It's becoming a problem."

The voice assured her that a truck would come as soon as possible.

Karen tried to focus on unpacking the master bedroom, lingering over the deep, mulled-wine scent of Ken's coats and the surprising softness of his socks. His clothes and shoes filled the closet. At this rate, there would be no room for hers. Not to mention her beads and jewelry-making tools. She'd have to keep those boxed up between projects now.

She called to Willie and said she was going to check the mail. Instead, she went out to her old Datsun and pulled a pack of Newports out of the canvas tote she kept in the trunk. She smoked two in a row, leaning against the side of the house, relishing the fact that Ken wasn't home to nag her. Still, she went through the motions of chewing the breath mints, spritzing the body spray and tucking everything back in the tote so he could go on thinking she only smoked one a day, after dinner. She squinted at the package on her way back inside. White, purple and orange blurred between her eyelashes. The colors of lilies.

She had beads in those colors—maybe she'd make a FedEx-inspired bracelet.

The package was still there at dusk. It was there the next morning and the one after that, and then she stopped looking.

Until one day she raised the blinds and there was a man sitting on the porch in its place, wearing a plaid work shirt and gray shorts. He had his back against the railing, his bare legs stretching the width of the top step. No shoes. She put a hand to her mouth. For a second she thought it was Willie's father, Jud. He had the same shaggy dark hair and heavy chin that seemed to weigh down the corners of his eyes. Except this man was several years older. There was no car in the driveway or on the street. He must have walked barefoot from wherever he'd come from.

He looked right at her, through her, and waved. It was the look Jud used to give her—the look that said I know more about you than you will ever know. The resemblance between the men hit a nerve. She reeled backward and struck her heel against a box of cookbooks she hadn't found a shelf for yet. She squatted below his line of vision, rubbing her foot. Maybe he hadn't really seen her, maybe he was just waving a bug away. She could stay hunched here all day. It would be all right. The TV would keep Willie occupied. Ken would be home from work in six hours, and if the man was still there by then, Ken would know what to do about it.

The doorbell rang.

Willie looked up from the TV, and Karen froze.

"Stay there," she said, and she waited until he turned back to the screen before she stood up. She checked that the security chain was in place and opened the door. The man peered in at her. He looked like Jud used to look when he was high. Dark, creased. He didn't speak.

"Bill Miller?" she finally asked.

He nodded and stumbled on the welcome mat.

"This is my house," he said.

"There was a package for you," she said, scanning the porch for the FedEx box.

"You don't belong here," he said.

"I called and told them to come get it."

"Come get it," he repeated.

"They must have come," she said.

He took a step toward the door, and she stepped back.

"I'm going to call the cops if you don't leave," she said.

"Don't leave."

"You don't belong here," she said.

"I used to," he said. "I belonged to you."

She slammed the door and turned the deadbolt. Her hands were shaking when she reached for the phone, and she dropped it twice before she could dial 911 and tell them to come get the crazy man off the porch.

Willie came and stood beside her, asking what was going on. She picked him up, straining under his weight, and watched through the peephole as the man paced in front of the door. He tripped over the welcome mat again, picked it up and threw it like a Frisbee into the yard.

"We know that man," Willie said. He meant it as a question, but it didn't sound that way.

"No, we don't." She was glad Willie had inherited her features, so she saw her own broad cheeks and hazel eyes when she looked at him.

The man staggered along the boxwoods, snapping off the dry branches as he must have done when he lived here. He was standing in the grass with a handful of dead twigs when the squad car pulled into the driveway.

She called Ken when it was over, but she waited until they were in bed that night before talking about it in detail. "It's weird—he made me feel like I was the one trespassing," she said. "Like I'm the one who's out of place here." She tried to laugh it off, knowing it must sound strange.

"This isn't his house anymore. He doesn't have any right to be here."

"Neither do I, when you look at it that way." She closed her eyes. It was a warm night, and she started to sweat where his skin touched hers. She was still getting used to his freckles. She used to wonder about the ones that showed on his forearms when he wore short sleeves. They continued up his body the way she thought, but the shoulders were thinner than she'd imagined.

She'd worked in the warehouse most of her adult life, until the layoffs. Fifty thousand square feet. They stored and shipped brochures and other materials for small businesses like WorkWare, Ken's software company. Fulfillment, it was called. She couldn't have told you what it was when she applied for the job ten years ago. *What makes you want to work in fulfillment?* the manager had asked in her interview. She said she liked being useful. She was good at alphabetizing and organization. Or she used to be, before she had to think about things like tie clips. Would she file them under the letter T or C? Would he want them on the shelf near his ties, or on the dresser by the mirror?

"This house wouldn't be right without you. And Willie."

In addition to the bed, he'd bought Willie a tricycle and a tee-ball set. He talked about taking him to high-school football games in the fall. When Willie started in with one of his tantrums, Ken talked him out of his fury with promises of milkshakes and movies. He was a born negotiator. A real businessman.

"We'll build that family room," Ken said, squeezing his arm around her. "By the end of summer it'll really feel like *ours*."

"A family room," she repeated. It sounded foreign. Ken had told her he got the idea for the extra room the first time he saw the house with its cramped living room. Had he already been thinking they'd move in together at that point? Otherwise, what family did he have in mind? Maybe any kind would do. She could feel how much he wanted it, how much he needed to make up for lost time, lost relationships.

I belonged to you.

Jud used to work at the warehouse, too, long before Ken became a client. She and Jud teamed up on the big projects. He picked, she packed. He'd toss paperclips at her, and sometimes he made faces behind the manager's back to make her laugh. They'd do dramatic, suggestive readings of the cover letters as they stuffed envelopes. *Thank you for contacting us*, they said. *We look forward to discussing your neeeeeds.*

They smoked together on breaks, ate lunch together, and after a while she started going home with him a couple nights a week. She was just getting into beading then, and she made him a keychain for his birthday. They broke up two weeks later. And now four years had gone by. She used to think about him all the time, and was glad when his presence in her head eventually faded. But now it was back like a punishment she deserved.

One day she bought some pansies on sale in the grocery store parking lot. When Willie got up from his nap, she brought him out to help plant the flowers around the mailbox like her grandmother used to.

"I want a roof on my bed," Willie said.

"A canopy?" The girl in one of his favorite cartoons had one over her bed.

"And walls, so it's like my own house."

Ken's house was on a fairly busy street—a lot of people used it as a shortcut to get to the main road—so she had to be careful when she was digging along the curb. She was aware of the people driving past, what they must be seeing when they looked at her.

She smiled, wanting to appear happy. You had to be happy if you were planting pansies.

"And a light for inside my house," Willie said.

Another set of wheels approached, but this time the sound slowed to a grind of gravel. She looked up to see a truck stopping alongside her. The window lowered. It was Bill.

"I don't mean to scare you," he said, holding up a hand that could have been Jud's. "I just want to apologize for showing up here last week and making a scene." As if he knew how often she'd replayed it in her mind. Willie stared.

"I was confused, forgot I don't live here anymore," he said. "I don't even remember it. Turns out I was having a diabetic episode." It sounded like a TV show. "I haven't been managing my insulin very well lately, but I'm doing better now."

She remembered the FedEx box from the pharmaceutical company. "I think your medicine was delivered here."

"Well, it won't happen again. I changed the address."

She hoped that was it, but he kept talking.

"I also wanted to thank you. When the police brought me down to the station, they saw my medical bracelet and took me to the hospital." He raised his arm and a silver chain slid on his thick wrist. "I might be dead otherwise. So. Thank you."

Willie closed the fingers of one hand around his other arm.

"I'm glad you're okay," she said, and she was. It was something she would say if she ran into Jud one of these days. If he was okay.

Bill put the truck into drive and she watched him leave, wondering if he'd been waiting to catch her outside in the yard to tell her all of that. Did that mean he'd been driving past the house all week, looking for her? She used to wish Jud would come looking for her, back when she still lived in her old place. She pushed the last pansy into the dirt and went inside, leaving the trowel on the porch.

Later that night she thought about Bill as she threaded silver beads onto a strand of wire. Everyone should wear a message telling the world what they need. The TV chattered in the next room, and she pictured Ken reclined in front of it. It bothered her that she couldn't tell if he was awake or not. She used to know what Ken needed—four-color letterhead, yellow envelopes, plenty of advance notice when it was time to restock. At dinner, she'd told him about Bill and the diabetes and explained that there was nothing to worry about. But she couldn't stop thinking about how much Bill looked like Jud, reminding her of how much wrong she'd done. She twisted the end of the wire to hold the beads in place and tucked it away in her jewelry box, hoping she was done with Bill Miller for good.

But she wasn't. Bill showed up again on a Saturday. Ken had taken Willie outside to play so Karen could do some job hunting online. When she finally gave up, she went to the window and nearly cried out when she noticed the truck in the driveway. Ken and Bill were standing in the front yard with bottles of beer, gesturing at the utility flags left from the property survey. "Our friend," Ken had been calling him, always with a sarcastic tone. Like, "Our *friend* didn't leave us the key to the shed." The man had left a half-dozen other keys, some that didn't seem to go to anything, but not the one they needed. Now the two men looked like old buddies—Ken in his confident red polo and Bill in a Punk Button concert T-shirt—talking and gesturing as if they did this every weekend. Suddenly the men turned and began walking toward the house with Willie between them like a favorite nephew. Karen ran into the kitchen and waited until they were inside before she came back around the corner.

Bill held his hand out to her, and she hesitated before shaking it. He was taller than Ken, and broader.

"Bill brought the shed key," Ken said. He liked to be in control of everything, even this.

"I live closer to you than the realtor, so I figured I'd just drop it off," Bill said. "There's a grill in the shed. Can't have it at the apartment, so it's yours now."

"He's going to stay for dinner and show us how to use it," Ken said.

"Great," Karen said, forcing a smile. She almost offered Bill a drink, but then remembered he already had one. How do you make someone feel at home when it's not your home? "Please— have a seat." The words sounded forced.

Ken shook his head. "We're going to the store to pick out some steaks. Need anything?"

She looked from one man to the other. "No."

Willie tugged on the cuff of her shorts, begging to go along.

"If they don't mind," she said. Ken nodded and held his hand up for a high-five from the boy. She used to think it was cute, this camaraderie, but it was starting to feel like a joke at her expense.

"I'll just use the bathroom first," Bill said. "Guess I don't need to ask where it is." He winked at Karen as he walked past, and her face flushed.

"I think he's going to build us that family room," Ken said. "He used to work in construction. And his dad was a contractor. Bill helped him build this house, if you can believe that."

"Sounds like you have a new friend," Karen said.

Ken smiled and shrugged. "He's out of work and could use the money. Plus, it's kind of nice to know the person who's always lived here. He can probably tell us a lot."

"Probably." She pictured Bill eating cereal in the dining area and watching TV in the same corner of the living room where Ken liked to sit.

When they left for the store, she stood in the middle of the room for a moment, surrounded by unpacked boxes. The crack in the east wall made the shape of a Y—like the "YES" option on the reply cards she used to send with letters from the warehouse. *YES! I'd like to know more about what you can do for me!* She traced the shape on her arm.

That night the four of them sat on the cement slab behind the house long after they finished eating. Someone down the street was burning leaves, and the smell overpowered what was left of the steaks and potatoes. Bill's insulated medical pouch sat on the plastic table like a disclaimer, a reminder of the first time she met him.

"Tell us more about the house," Ken said.

"You already know it," Bill said. "Full disclosure and all."

"There's got to be more. I want all the details."

Willie scooted his chair closer to Ken's. Karen was surprised at how comfortable Willie was with Ken, how quickly he was adjusting to their new life.

Bill sighed and leaned back in his chair. "Well, the floor slopes in the kitchen. The cabinet by the stove doesn't shut good, and the pantry shelves aren't level. The stairs creak. But I'm sure you figured all that out already."

Karen hadn't even noticed the slope in the kitchen. She wondered if that meant the floorboards were rotting.

"And I had to patch a hole in the wall from where my wife threw a bag of potatoes from across the room." He laughed. "She wasn't always that way. It was really good before it got bad."

Karen had a sudden flash of two bodies entangled in the bedroom where she now slept with Ken.

"We built this house when I was sixteen, but I didn't really live here till I inherited it when I was thirty-five and married, like you."

Ken glanced at Karen.

"They aren't married," Willie said, laughing.

Ken looked at Karen again. "Someday."

Karen stacked the dirty plates and pushed them to a corner of the table. "I'm surprised you were willing to give up the house," she said.

"It wasn't my choice," Bill said. "It just worked out that way. Like most things." His eyes connected with hers and stayed there until she turned her head.

She used to tell people Jud had left her, but he'd just left on vacation. An annual fishing trip with his uncle. It was August, and business was slow. Their biggest client was a consulting firm in town, and its VP of sales stopped by the office late one day looking for her boss, but he was gone too. Karen was the only one there, manning the phones even though no one was calling. The VP had box seats for that night's ballgame—maybe she'd like to go since no one else was around? She thought she might, so she did. And the next day when he asked, she thought she might let him buy her dinner. He said he liked how agreeable she was. From then on, she sneaked out through the loading dock most days at noon and took her lunch break with him. When Jud got back it took him a couple days to figure out what was going on, and once he did he quit. Later, when the VP lost interest, Karen thought about tracking down Jud to tell him she was having his baby, but she'd heard he took a job teaching English somewhere in Asia. He wouldn't have been a good father anyway. And besides, finding him would mean owning up to the fact that she'd hurt the only man who'd ever really cared for her.

The next afternoon Karen opened the mailbox and found a piece of notebook paper folded in half and frayed on one side from its spiral binding. She opened it up and read:

Dear Karen and Ken,

Here's your official project quote. Looking forward to working for you.

Thanks,
Bill

A dollar amount followed. She was surprised at how low it was, as well as the neatness of his handwriting. She'd expected to see something more like Jud's scrawl.

She gave Ken the quote that night, and he took it upstairs to his desk. She stayed at the kitchen table, coloring with Willie on a scratch pad. "Dear Karen," she wrote in green crayon. She studied the letters and scribbled over them.

That night Ken put his arm around her in bed.

"You think we might get married someday?" he asked, running a finger along the curve of her breast.

"I don't know."

"You didn't say anything when it came up last night."

"I just don't want to ruin what we have," she said. People said that about relationships sometimes. She wondered what it was they had, exactly. But without it, she had nothing.

He kissed her. She opened herself and let him in. He was gentle, pausing after every movement to emphasize its importance. She was good at making it seem like she got what she needed out of this. With her eyes closed, she almost did.

Bill started coming over once or twice a week to talk about the family room. He and Ken sat at the table mapping out specs, applying for permits and putting together a calendar. The project would take most of the summer, but that was fine. Ken was in no rush. He didn't want Bill to work on weekends except for breakthrough day—when they'd break through the side of the house to connect the addition—so Ken could be home to help.

Karen listened to their plans while she read stories to Willie in his new bed behind the sheet Ken had hung from the ceiling for him. Willie liked to be tucked in, hidden. He was used to a three-room apartment, so Ken's house probably seemed like too much space to him. She could sympathize.

Most evenings, once Willie was asleep and Ken was watching the news, she took his laptop upstairs to bed and searched for jobs. She typed up a cover letter explaining how much she loved working in a warehouse. Then another one explaining how much she would love to work in an office. And another that said she would love to work with children. She made a bracelet using fifty-two small beads of different colors and clasped it around her wrist. One for every week of the year, she realized. She'd already been living with Ken for twelve weeks. She counted clockwise to the twelfth bead and saw that it was red. She counted to twelve going the other way, and that bead was black. She went to bed and lay awake for a long while, fingering the beads and listening to the murmur of the TV.

The family-room project began on a Monday, when Ken was at work. Bill showed up alone in a faded red T-shirt and frayed jeans. His truck was piled with tools and lumber.

"Guess I'll leave you to it," Karen said. She checked that all the doors and windows were locked and then took Willie along for a day of errands. When she ran out of things on her list, they went to the park. When the park got too hot, they went to the mall and stayed until dinnertime.

She and Willie stayed away from the house the next day, too, and the day after that. It felt like a full-time job. By four o'clock on Friday, she was exhausted and headed home. She was relieved to see that Bill's truck was gone. When she checked the mail, she found another piece of notebook paper like the first, but this one was wrapped around a box of Girl Scout cookies.

Dear Karen,

Ordered these from my niece, but I can't eat them.

Bill

PS: You don't have to leave when I'm here. I won't bother you.

Her face flushed to think he knew she was avoiding him. This was a peace offering. She looked at the note again. *Dear Karen.* She put it in her pocket. The paper folded against her hip.

That night she woke up around two in the morning, thinking of Jud. *I need you, Karen.* He was the only one who'd ever said such a thing to her. She went downstairs to the kitchen and stood at the window overlooking the patch of dirt where the family room would go. Bill had dug up a couple of bushes and filled the yard with wood and tools. The lumber looked familiar in the moonlight, like pallets of product waiting to be scanned and shelved. She pulled the Girl Scout cookies from the back of the pantry where she'd hidden them and ate the entire box. They were the kind with chocolate, caramel and coconut—her favorite. She drank half the bottle of wine from Denise. Then she went outside and arranged the tools in a neat row along the back of the house, in alphabetical order. Bucket. Hammer. Level. Nails. Saw. Screwdriver. Tape Measure. Wrench. She picked up the hammer and felt the wood's smoothness from Bill's grip.

Over the weekend she ran into Denise at the mailbox.

"I can't believe you're letting Bill Miller do that work for you," Denise said.

"It wasn't my choice," Karen said.

She stayed home Monday morning. When Bill arrived, she stepped out the back door and thanked him for the cookies.

"Did Willie like them?"

"Yes," she said.

She went back inside and glanced out at Bill throughout the morning. At noon, she let Willie eat SpaghettiOs in bed. She made two sandwiches. She left one on the counter and brought the second one out to Bill with a glass of water because she felt like she should. He was staring off into the distance, a measuring tape in one hand. When he heard the back door, he dropped the tape on the lawn and thanked her for the sandwich.

"Eat with me," he said. "Please." He sat on the grass next to his toolbox.

"I already ate," she said.

He pulled his medical bag out of his toolbox, and before she knew it he had lifted his shirt and given himself a shot of insulin. She wondered if she should turn away, but she didn't. His stomach wasn't as dark as his arms, and the hair wasn't as thick. She was glad he kept his shirt on while he worked. It was over in seconds. He took a bite of the sandwich and smiled at her. When Willie came outside, she wiped sauce off his cheek with her thumb.

"Did you know you and I have the same name?" Bill asked him. "William, right?"

The boy nodded.

"Bill is short for William, just like Willie is. It's a good name."

Willie grinned.

"Hey, I have something for you."

Bill went to his truck, dug in the toolbox and pulled out a light with a long, twisty neck.

"I found this when I was going through my storage unit," he said, holding the snake light out to the boy. "For your house. You can wrap it around the bedpost."

She didn't remember telling Bill that Willie thought of his bed as a house, that he wanted a light for it. It made her nervous to think Bill might have overheard a conversation when she didn't realize he was within earshot. The boy took the light and jumped up and down with excitement, winding the thing around his arm and then his leg. Karen pulled a cigarette out of her tote and lit it.

"You're not going to offer me one?" Bill asked.

"I didn't know you smoke."

"I do sometimes."

She offered the pack, and he pulled out a cigarette. They stood together, breathing the same haze.

"Ken hates that I do this," she said.

"I know." He took a long drag, and in that moment she felt the same tingling she used to feel around Jud—the thrill of smoking a joint on her lunch break, drinking her dinner, having sex in the bathroom of the movie theater. The thrill of being young and being broke and being numb and just not caring what happened next.

She thought Bill might kiss her, but he didn't. After a while he said he better get back to work, that he was starting the frame around the foundation today. Willie asked if he could watch, and she said no. But she watched—from the kitchen window. She scrubbed the sink. She took glasses out of the cabinets and wiped down the shelves and then put them back. Half the house remained in boxes, but she stood there and washed dishes that were already clean.

She began making him a sandwich every day at lunchtime. When she asked he said he preferred ham, so that's what she bought when she went to the store with Ken's credit card. Bill let Willie watch up close when he gave himself his insulin shot, and Willie said he wished he had diabetes so he could give himself shots, too. They ate sitting on the bare boards that would someday be the floor of the family room. She imagined that she was married to Bill and he was building this room for the three of them. What would they do in it? Watch movies? Put together puzzles? Play board games? When they finished eating, Bill and Karen smoked. When Ken came home each night, Bill came inside to give a quick progress report and use the bathroom. She was glad he never seemed to need it during the day. The idea of him pulling his pants down, the chance that she might walk in on him at any moment, was just too much for her to handle.

She listened from the other room the day Bill told Ken it was taking longer than he thought. A week later he said his measurements were off and he'd have to redo the wall on the south side. They'd have to postpone the breakthrough, but he wouldn't charge for the extra time.

She asked Ken how it was going, and he said pretty good.

He asked Karen how the unpacking was going, and she said pretty good.

The last wall went up. The roof appeared.

She wrote more cover letters. Applied for more jobs.

"Why don't you just come work for me?" Ken asked. "I could find a job for you." He brushed a strand of her hair behind her ear.

"I bet you could." But she didn't bring it up again.

"Karen. I don't know anything about you," Bill said one day at lunchtime. "Except that you have a son and you're not married."

She leaned against the side of the house where a door would eventually go, allowing passage in and out of the addition.

"What makes you happy?"

"A lot of things." She folded her napkin into a tidy square. "Willie."

"I carved my girlfriend's initials with mine in the attic wall when I was seventeen," he said.

"And I buried our dog under that tree, and then something came and dug it up."

Her eyes went to the tree.

"The night my parents died, I came here and slept in the grass."

"Why are you telling me all that?"

"Ken asked for the details about the house, and I guess I thought of a few more." He shrugged and finished his sandwich in silence.

"You know, you're really not doing a very good job here," she said, pointing to the nails at odd angles in the wood.

"I'm trying." He shrugged. "But I'm new at this."

"I thought you said you built this house."

"I did say that." He grinned. "Because I need the money. The tools were my dad's. He's the real carpenter. Not my fault if no one runs a background check."

He didn't ask her not to tell Ken. Somehow he knew he didn't need to.

Ken used to say he was a pretty good judge of character. He could figure out everything he needed to know just by looking at someone. But he'd told her once about a sales guy he'd hired who assaulted one of his secretaries, and it turned out the guy was a sex offender. And Ken had invited Karen to move in without even asking if she'd ever lived with another man before. She hadn't. Not technically. She was overqualified in some areas and completely inexperienced in others.

That night she brought dinner to the table, one item at a time.

She set a plate of pork chops in front of Ken. "I love traveling," she said, wondering if she would have gone to Asia with Jud if things had worked out differently. "The idea of it. But you know what? I've never even been on an airplane."

She brought the string beans. "I took two years of French in school, but my mother made me quit because she didn't think it was practical. I took typing instead."

She put bread and the butter dish at the edge of the table. "I was thirteen when the new boy next door came over to play." She glanced at Willie. "I was supposed to be nice to him. Even if he wasn't nice to me."

She sat down. The fork, knife and spoon made a family around her plate.

"Where'd all that come from?" He didn't say it unkindly.

"I realized there were some things you probably didn't know about me." She slid a pork chop onto Willie's plate and began cutting it for him. The knife skidded and shrieked.

"You can always tell me anything you want," Ken said, lowering his face. When he noticed she was still standing there, he looked up and met her eyes.

"But you never ask."

Jud used to ask. *What's brewing*, he used to say. *What's stewing? What's chewing?* And she'd gotten mad at him for it.

"You did a really good job on dinner," Ken said, chewing as he talked.

She waited for him in bed that night. When he didn't come up, she went downstairs, turned off the TV, and unbuttoned his pants. It had started this way between them, passionate, unexpected, the day she personally delivered samples of his new letterhead. This time, he pushed her head away.

Breakthrough happened on the first Saturday in August. Ken wanted French doors leading from the living room into the family room, so they needed to cut a big hole in a load-bearing wall. They started with a small one so they could make sure there weren't any pipes or wires in the way. Karen was sitting on the couch with Willie when the reciprocating saw whined and stabbed its way into the house. When the square of drywall fell to the floor, it covered the carpet in dust. Willie ran over and twirled his finger in it. Bill's face appeared in the hole like a framed picture on the wall, like an old lover looking in to see what had happened to her life. He waved at her and shined a flashlight into the innards of the house, searching, examining.

"We're in the clear," he said, stepping back.

It took the men all morning to measure and cut the hole for the door, put in the doorframe with a load-bearing header and set up temporary bracing. Around noon Karen made sandwiches—ham for Bill, roast beef for Ken, peanut butter for Willie and herself. Bill stepped into the bathroom with his insulin. Karen set out a bowl of apples, a bag of chips and a clamshell of cookies from the bakery Ken liked. She poured lemonade, set the table and told the men to come in. She was nervous. It felt strange to be eating together, all together, this way, with that gaping hole in the wall leading into a bright, empty memory of a room. She sat on the edge of her chair and busied herself with Willie, making sure he didn't eat too many chips, wiping up his crumbs, pouring a glass of milk to go with his cookie.

"You make a good sandwich," Bill said, as if she'd never made him one before. A smile crept across his face when Ken wasn't looking. She felt herself blush.

When she finished eating, she wanted a cigarette. It was part of the routine. But she could not, would not, stand outside, next to the shell of a family room, and smoke with Bill while Ken watched. Instead, she cleared the dishes and watched while Bill stepped out and smoked below the kitchen window. He looked up at her once and raised her tote bag in one hand. She must have left it in the yard. Her body needed the nicotine—her temples were pounding—but she shook her head once, quickly, and moved out of his view. He took another draw and stamped the butt out in the grass.

"Would you mind picking that up?" Ken asked when Bill came back inside. Ken was eating a cookie with one hand cupped under his chin.

"Say what?"

"Your cigarette butt."

"I hate to break it to you, but there's loads of them out there."

"Maybe you should pick them all up, then."

Bill looked at Karen, and she wanted to run out and clean the yard herself. "Don't worry. When I'm done here, I'll clean everything up so there'll be no trace of me."

Not possible.

"I don't mean to be a hard-ass, I just think it's disrespectful," Ken said. "Smokers never understand nonsmokers."

"I'm sure Karen would agree with that," Bill said. With the food put away and the dishes washed, there was nothing left for Karen to do but stand between the men. She looked for Willie, hoping he might need something, but he was running circles in the empty family room.

"Oh they're yours," Ken said, finally understanding. "Both of yours." He looked from one to the other of them.

Karen cleared her throat. "I always pick mine up," she said.

"See? There's never been a trace of her," Bill said.

"Well," Ken said. "Good."

"I'll clean up the yard," Bill said, "after we put in the doors."

Bill nailed some small boards into the jamb as temporary supports and squeezed caulk into the crack between the living room and family room floors. He held one side of the double doors and motioned for Ken to hold the other. They were beautiful—dark red mahogany with ten glass panes per door and a pair of simple nickel handles where they met in the middle. A heavy protective film covered the glass on both sides, diffusing the light.

Something slipped and Bill struggled under the weight. "You're going to have to do better than that, cowboy," he said.

Ken set his end down with a thud and let go, planting his feet wide apart. Bill had to reach up and brace the doors to keep them from falling on top of him. "Then tell me what to do."

Even with Bill standing on the bare floorboards of the family room and Ken on the higher plane of the living room, it was clear how much bigger Bill was. It looked like the doors were a part of him, like the retractable wings on one of Willie's robots.

"Lift them up again and hold them steady." Bill kept his voice low and firm.

Karen couldn't see Willie—he was inside the unfinished family room, on the other side of the doors with Bill.

"That's what I was doing," Ken said.

Bill ignored him. "Put the bottom in first, and then ease it into place."

The doors didn't fit.

"Hold it," Bill said.

Ken stepped back.

"Hold *the doors*. I need to shave a little off the side." The sander shrilled, and Bill guided it along the edge of the door. When that didn't do it, Bill took the sander to the doorframe. On the fourth try, the doors eased into place.

"You're not used to someone else being in charge, are you?" Bill asked, driving a screw through a hinge. The drill made a tired grinding noise and stopped. He opened one of the doors stiffly, stepped through to join Ken and Karen in the living room, and forced the door shut behind him.

"Not when the person in charge can't actually take control of the situation," Ken said. "You have to be more clear about what needs to be done."

"Well, if you put it that way," Bill said, "I'd have to think about where to even start."

Ken stared at him.

"Stop," Karen said before she realized it. "Stop running in there, Willie." She didn't really care if he was running.

"Oh he's fine," Ken said, annoyed.

"There's *a lot* that could be done around here," Bill said, reaching for another screw.

"It's not that bad," Ken said.

"I'm not talking about the house." Bill lowered the drill. "And I don't think you really want me in control of *this* situation."

"The situation?"

"Those were your words."

"This is *my* family room, and it's for *my* family."

"Is it."

"Look, I don't know what you're trying to get at, but I'm pretty sure it's none of your business."

"He's right, you know," Karen said.

"See?" Ken said, stepping toward Karen.

She could have let Ken think she was taking his side. He would have liked that.

"I meant—there's a lot that could be done," she said. She could start selling her bracelets online. She could get Denise to babysit so she could go to that career fair she heard about on the radio. She could stop letting other people make her decisions for her. "We should fix the cabinet by the stove, for starters. And it wouldn't be too hard to replace those old pantry shelves."

"You can do whatever you want," Bill said, glaring at Ken. "It's your house."

"That's right, and you'd better not forget that," Ken said.

"Nothing is going on between me and her, if that's what you're thinking," Bill said, pointing at Karen. She couldn't believe he'd actually said those words, as if he'd known all along that she'd expected something to happen. And Ken probably had, too. "Nothing would *ever* happen there."

She was looking at Bill when they heard the bang. She was trying to figure out if he meant he wasn't attracted to her, or if he meant he wouldn't cheat with another man's girlfriend even though it would have been so easy. All those long days alone together, the big quiet bedroom just a few steps away. It stunned her. *Nothing would ever happen there.* Why not? She didn't know how to be near a man who needed something from her—he did, she was sure of it—but never even asked.

The bang.

She might not have said yes.

It sounded like a shotgun, and then the sound of glass shattering on the other side of the French doors, where Willie had been playing by himself. And then silence.

Her boy, on the other side of those doors.

Karen shoved past Bill—looking back, she would realize this was the only time she ever touched him—but the doors didn't budge. She grabbed both handles and shook them up and down, straining to see through the film covering the windows and feeling the entire broad plane of glass and wood shake on the one hinge Bill had installed. She barely noticed the cracking sound— wood splintering in the doorjamb from the force of her pulling. Then she felt the lock under her palm and paused long enough to turn, turn, turn it, her fingers shaking, and burst through to where Willie sat on the bare floor where he and she and Bill had shared so many lunches, the nail gun in his hands.

Karen pulled the fingers away from the trigger, shoving the thing aside, and splayed the hands in her own, looking for blood, expecting blood, but his hands, his face, his arms were fine. It was just the window he'd aimed at and shot into the yard, but even the glass had gone out and away and left him unscarred. He was crying then, just from the shock of it, and so was she, and she picked him up and held him.

An hour later, there was a knock at the front door. Two soft raps meant for her ears. She glanced toward the living room, but Ken had gone upstairs to take a shower, and she'd tucked Willie into bed. She could open the door if she wanted to. She cupped her hand around the doorknob and held it, leaning her cheek against the wood until she could almost feel Bill's breath from the other side. It was only later, after his footsteps retreated, after the engine started, after the truck pulled away—only then did she turn the knob and peer out after him. On the other side of the doorknob hung the tote bag full of all the things she used to hide how much she smoked, a single sunny dandelion dangling from the lip.

She stood outside Willie's room and listened to the deep sighs of his snoring. Nudging the door open, she studied the glow coming from behind the sheet-wall. His secret little world, a planet glowing in space. She tiptoed across the room and peered inside like she was standing on the sidewalk, looking in on a stranger. Willie slept sideways on the bed in a nest of blankets. His teddy bears lined the wall, their glass eyes glinting in the sheen of the snake light wound around the bedpost. He'd stacked books in one corner, his toy robots in the other. A half-eaten graham cracker lay beside his pillow. Along the foot of the bed, he'd layered a dozen juice boxes like bricks, forming a low wall. With a sudden, sharp pain, she wished she had been the one to hang the sheet and give him the snake light.

Karen wasn't sure Bill would show up Monday morning, but he did.

"Do you need anything?" she asked.

"I just need to get this done." His face was long and haggard. He hadn't shaved.

She thought about leaving for the day, taking Willie to the park or the mall to get away from the uncomfortable silence. But now that the breakthrough had happened, she couldn't leave. She couldn't leave Bill alone in the house.

Willie sat on the couch while Bill fixed the broken window and the splintered doorjamb and installed the wood flooring. An electrician was scheduled to come in a couple days, and he and Bill would put in a ceiling fan. Next would come crown molding and paint—Ken wanted a soft shade of yellow. There was still a lot to do, enough to keep Bill busy for another week or two. Karen lingered in the kitchen. She made a broccoli salad and a tuna salad and chocolate cupcakes, all the while watching the man and the boy. It felt strange to look up from her chopping and mixing to see Bill inside the house. He stayed focused on his work, and she stayed focused on hers.

They didn't speak, so Willie did. She leaned close to hear. He told Bill the names of the bears in his bed. Blue, Green, Ken Junior, Bill Junior and Junior Junior. He said he wanted Bill to play ball with him when he was done working. And now that Bill could come inside, he could come upstairs and see the house in his bedroom. Willie said his mom was going to marry Ken and that Ken said they were going to go camping in the fall and get a dog someday and go sledding on the street in winter and that his fifth birthday was coming up and he wanted Bill to come to the party and sit next to him when he blew out his candles, Bill on one side and Ken on the other.

He has no idea what I want for us, she thought.

She meant Willie, and she meant Ken, and she meant Bill and Jud and everyone else along the way.

The cupcakes were in the oven. The salads were chilling. She was out of things to do for Ken and Willie and Bill. She checked the pantry and the refrigerator and started a grocery list on the back of an envelope. Things We Need. This she could handle. Applesauce. Bananas. Chips. What else? She'd thought of something she needed that started with D, but now she couldn't remember what it was. Doughnuts? Deli meat? Dear Karen.

Diet Coke. She was out of Diet Coke.

Eggs. Flour. Graham crackers. Ham. Ice cream.

And a job.

She stopped and held the pen for a long while. Then she put it down. Something was pressing into her hip, so she reached into her pocket, the one where she'd put the Dear Karen letter, and pulled out her lighter. She lit a cigarette and blew a long stream of smoke into the kitchen before she realized she was breaking Ken's rule. Then she put the cigarette between her lips and breathed in again.

She used to wonder what would happen when Bill finished the addition, what she'd do the first day he didn't show up. Now she only wondered how Willie would adjust to not having him around all the time. But he'd manage. Just as he'd adjusted to Ken and his house. They'd both be fine on their first day alone in the house with the completed family addition. Maybe she'd take Willie to the pool or a museum or the zoo. Maybe they wouldn't be in the house at all. Maybe they'd be much farther gone by then.

How Far Gone

The spaniel ran up and showed me her shaved temple, the bare skin like a patch of walked-on bubblegum with stitches down the middle. I've seen worse, I said. This is a hell of a long way from Fallujah. The women following her wore the colors of the Imperial Gangsters. They moved like gangsters, too, but in spandex and sandals. My reflex was to look for heat on their thighs. You can never be too careful, even at a suburban dog park.

It was a cyst, the tan woman said, pointing to the spaniel. We had to have it removed. She asked which one is mine, and it took me a second to realize she meant which dog. I pointed to the empty path and said she must have run ahead. The women wanted to talk about training, of all things, a word that brought to mind Camp Lejeune and all things basic. They walked with me, their arms around each other's hips. Can yours sit? Stay? Lie down?

The come is the hardest part, the pale one said, and I laughed. I thought that was supposed to be easy for you. I almost said it. But I stayed focused on the ghost of Lila's Dalmatian. I was hungry, seeing spots, willing the animal to appear in the brush, Lila at her side. They'd left four days ago, the morning after I blacked out and couldn't explain where I'd been. *Come. Come back home.* As much as I hated Lila's mother, I had to give her credit for tipping me off that Lila was here. When I got off the bus and found our old Datsun parked by the dogshit bin, I bent and kissed the fender.

"All right, I have to ask," the tan woman said. "Where's your membership card? You know you have to pay to bring your dog here."

"I got my own dog tags," I said, patting my chest, hoping for a laugh.

"I can have you removed," she said. Like a cyst. Or a bad memory. She held up a cell phone. "I know a cop."

"*I'm* a cop," I said, and she dropped her arm. "I'm looking for someone."

"We don't want any trouble," she said.

"We're in agreement on that," I said. I could almost see Lila's face in the pattern of the leaves. She looked good with green hair, honeysuckle tucked behind her ears. I realized then that I hadn't shaved since Lila ran off, and I was still wearing camo swim trunks and a work shirt stained with egg. No wonder they were suspicious.

"I'm not arresting anyone," I said. "I'm looking for my girl-friend. She has the membership card, but she forgot her keys." It sounded domestic, reasonable. "She asked me to bring them to her," I added.

They nodded, but even they somehow knew Lila could never *forget* her keys. She had an enormous tangle of them, like a metal Chihuahua, and felt naked without the weight on her arm. That's what she told me the night I met her, when I stole them to keep her from leaving a party. I was mixing drinks, and she said she'd rather have a mixed metaphor, so I made her a deep blue sea breeze that looked like an oil spill on the rocks. I dared her to drink it down, and she did, and another after that. I told her there's no limit to the world you can create in a glass, like a habi-tat for a cricket you catch in the weeds.

I also told her that if you line up all the bottles I drink in a year, they'd go around the world nineteen times. If you put all the dogs in the world nose to ass they'd only wrap around four-teen times. But if you line up all the things that go missing every year—people and words and understanding—they'd fill their own universe, from the sun to Pluto and on to the planet no one even knows about yet.

A collie ran up behind me and wiped its face on my leg. I reached down and pinched its lip until it whimpered. I smiled at the owner and twirled my key ring on my finger. If Lila's keys were a Chihuahua, mine were its neutered nuts on a sphincter. One went to the Datsun and the other to our apartment, and they rattled together at a high-pitched frequency only Lila could hear. That's what I was thinking when I finally saw her, so I have to believe it's true. The lesbians chased their spaniel, the dick leashed his collie, and Lila rounded the bend with her face turned toward the woods, listening.

"I found you," I said, pressing her arm like a button on an elevator. It was like finding a good knife on a dead body or bread in a house you thought had been looted days ago. Like waking up alive in the desert. She didn't seem surprised to see me. I took that as a good sign.

"I lost Elly," she said. It was short for Ellipsis.

"Where did you last see her?" I asked.

"Right here," she said, holding out her hands, cupping the phantom face with its inky fingerprints that could be traced back to both of us. So much had slipped through those fingers. Second and third and fourth chances. I'd last seen Elly looking out the window, watching me leave.

"Maybe she got out when someone opened the gate," I said. She was always looking for an excuse to run. The look on Lila's face scared me. "But maybe she's still inside."

Lila was doing that thing she does where she musters courage from her throat, swallowing, holding up her chin like it hurt to talk. "Either way, she can't be too far gone."

And maybe, then, neither can we. I know what too far looks like. It looks like a man falling asleep in his own urine with the moon in his mouth. A man who can't tell if his heart's still beating until someone smells his groin. A man who bites his tongue and throws up egg on his shirt. And yet here I am. I thought I knew what too far looked like, but there is no such thing.

She isn't going to ask where I was when I blacked out, or where I've been these last four days. At least not now. This is how I'll always remember us: walking with my arm around her hip, hanging on tight. The lesbians make it look so easy. We're calling now, the two of us together, rattling keys—her keys, my keys, our keys—and looking for something as familiar as our own finger-prints, swirled one inside the other. *Come.* Listening for words we know but won't say, straining to hear the panting, milk-bone sigh that means I'm tired and I want to go home—or as close as you'll take me.

Acknowledgments

Many of these stories started at Bennington College, where I learned how to trust myself as a writer. I'm forever grateful to my teachers for their wisdom and encouragement, especially Amy Hempel, Bret Anthony Johnston, Alice Mattison, Brian Morton, and Lynne Sharon Schwartz.

Thank you to Andy Briseño and Colin Winnette for seeing something good in these pages, and to the entire team at the University of North Texas Press who brought this book to life, especially Karen DeVinney and Bess Whitby.

My deepest thanks go to the editors who previously published nine of the twelve stories in this collection. The title story, "Orders of Protection," appeared in *AGNI Online* in July 2013. "A Thousand Needle Stings" appeared in the spring/summer 2016 issue of *West Branch Wired*. "Another Round" and "A+ Electric" appeared in the fall 2011 issue of *Meridian*. "Step Off at Ten" appeared in the spring 2012 issue of *Salamander*. "An Hour You Don't Expect" appeared in the spring 2017 issue of *Fifth Wednesday Journal*. (Vern Miller and Jim Ballowe, thank you for believing in me.) "The Ice River History Museum, Formerly Saint Catherine's Convent" appeared in Volume 62, number 1 of *Shenandoah* and won an honorable mention for the Bevel Summers Prize for the Short Short Story. "Ozone" appeared in the summer 2018 issue of the *Rappahannock Review*. Finally, "How Far Gone" appeared in the summer/fall 2012 issue of *Free State Review*.

To all my family and friends, near and far: Thank you for inspiring and supporting me, always.

And to Scott, Dell, and Eleanor: You are the other legs of this table, my everything. I'm so grateful for you.